Wolseley

J. John le Grange

"A profoundly affective novel brimming with solid writing that delves into the darker corners of being human."- *Kirkus Reviews*

"The author brings a different perspective to apartheid's aftermath, introducing a "white" world riddled with hopelessness." - *Times Live*

Wolseley

ISBN-13: 978-0-620-62363-6

ISBN-10: 0-620-62363-2

ASIN: B00MNU5T6A

2nd edition. Published by South Africa Writing

Johannesburg, Cape Town

www.zawriting.com

This book is dedicated

to

Nicola E

and

Jennifer C and Cheryl C

- who reminded me to live

Before we begin...

I know that this story is difficult to take in but it is one that, I believe, needs to be shared.

I am a South African and I am most thankful for having been born in the most beautiful country in the world. Thankful to have had the love and grace of two mothers, my biological mother and Gladys, so very much more than 'the *maid.*' Thankful to have witnessed an extraordinary transition and the restoration of dignity to so many.

This is why I have written this book - to reflect on the essence of dignity and to remind myself of the many challenges that are still a part of this country called South Africa. Challenges that are not about race, but the impairment of dignity.

The words in italics reflect our uniquely South African language, our 'isms'. A 'dictionary' can be found at the back of this book, which includes words like *robot* - a traffic light anywhere else in the world - and a flavour of our shared identity.

Thank you for coming on this journey with me.

J. John le Grange

Part 1-House

0.

"Jesus, Pa! What are we going to do?" she shrieked.

"Magda, do not use the Lord's name in vain," her father said, looking displeased and confused.

"Sorry, Pa...but he said we have to leave at the end of the month...where will we go?" Her voice was breaking as she tried to get the words out.

"I will sort it out. I always do." He didn't know why he had said that. Maybe he needed convincing at this time, too.

He looked at her trying to comfort her but he knew that his face gave away the truth: they were in trouble.

"We will have to pray for the Lord to protect us." A statement, a solution.

Hendrik, the man of the house, would have to let Martha, the breadwinner, know of the news...and pray like he had never prayed before.

1.

Wolseley, like the person after whom it is named, is not particularly attractive. It has neither the beauty of Franschhoek nor the reputation of Stellenbosch. It is an afterthought on the way to Ceres.

You know that you are nearing your destination when you are hit with a smell, one so potent and real that it creeps into your nostrils and reminds you that this is fruit country, and that rotting fruit in late summer is what feeds commerce in this part of the world.

The town is small, one main road, houses and some processing plants for wood. An earthquake once ripped through the area leaving in its wake various destroyed homes and some of those still standing are made without bricks and clay, temporary accommodation that somehow became permanent.

On the outskirts of the town, after taking a right at the 7-Eleven and crossing a bridge, there behind the train tracks and ensconced into the industrial part of town are three small cottages.

The house is not in the residential area of Wolseley, nor in its centre. Further up and within sight of the cottages is the *township* or *location* where black and *coloured* people live. Apartheid may have ended but poverty still segregates.

It is a humble house with fencing around it, not the fancy type with bars, but a simple metal fence, with a small gate that squeaks when it opens. The windows of the house are covered with wire netting metallic bars that masquerade as a security feature. They are not tastefully done but look rather messy, just like cages for chickens that have been placed over the windows so as not to let the livestock out. The house is dark, even during the day when the sun is at its brightest.

In the front of the house is a small verandah from which can be seen the surrounding mountains from afar – and the wood pulping plant nearby. Its floor is painted red. Over the years the paint has worn away and so it looks patchy and speckled. If this were Tuscany it would be called weathered – which is romantic – except in Wolseley it is derelict, and neither romantic nor charming.

The house itself is a dirty cream, and its roof red, like the verandah. It is set on a large plot on which there is also a dilapidated stable where horses must have once been kept. This rather rickety structure is no longer steady – the current owner, like the previous ones, has not bothered to knock it down. It remains intact and a remnant of a more glorious past. To call what the house has a garden would be a misnomer, for, although the plot is large and covered in grass and many riotous plants, it is a neglected, abandoned space which, coupled with the state of the house, tells a story to all who pass by it on the dirt road that fronts it.

2.

"He has sold the house," Kevin said as a matter of fact, "and he wants you out of here by the time transfer takes place which is at the end of the month."

Hendrik had looked at him, uncertain.

"But he can't evict us," Hendrik had argued. "We have rights."

"Listen, Mr. Van der Walt, you owe six months in rent and you are lucky that the owner has not called the Sherriff of the Court to attach your goods," Kevin said, in a tone that conveyed this was not open to negotiation.

"Come on. Please, man. My wife is the only one working at this time, we have nowhere to go..." Hendrik said, looking down.

"That is unfortunate, Mr. Van der Walt, but you have to be out at the end of the month, so it is time to get your affairs in order."

"We just need more time, can he not consider giving us one more month, please I am begging you." His desperation was alarming.

Kevin knew that the best thing to do in a situation like this was to go. Pointless staying around to have a discussion around something that was set in stone. With that he nodded his head at Mr. Van der Walt and walked through the gate, closing it firmly behind him before climbing in his car.

Only when the house was visible in the distance, in his rear view mirror, did he let out a sigh of relief.

That house was cursed. Never before in his twenty years in the real estate business had he ever experienced anything like it. He had sold it to different clients four times in one year. The first client had wormed his way out of the deal after his wife had come to look at the house and complained that it was too close to the *township*. The second had bought it after seeing its picture on the Internet, the property had just transferred. Then came the news that it had been broken into. Even with burglar bars on each window 'they' had got through the security gate. The new owners did not even bother to move in. The house was left vacant. Finally he was instructed to sell it again, this time as quickly as possible. He had advertised it in the Cape Town paper as a 'country escape' and sold it the next weekend to an artsy gay type who had come with his designer boyfriend to look it over. He had signed the offer to purchase in Kevin's car, as he had to get back to Cape Town for an urgent meeting.

When it transferred he had followed the instructions and found what he thought was a suitable tenant. The family was new in town, looking for somewhere to stay urgently but with a low rent. He had not bothered doing any checks, they looked decent and paid the one-month deposit and first month's rent. They moved in the next weekend.

That was the first and last time any money had been paid. He was left with egg on his face. The owner was not happy, and although he never accused Kevin directly of being responsible for this situation, every time he spoke to him he would ask what solution he could offer.

Kevin had visited the house at least twice a month to request a payment. It was the same each time. Excuses, excuses and more excuses. The woman was the worst at lying, she always said, "Next time we will have something for you."

Then came the phone call that he knew was bound to happen.

"Sell it and get them out," the owner had said. Clearly the ceiling of irritation and *bond* costs had been reached.

"Please, consider a few more months," he heard himself saying. "You will be putting them onto the street."

"That is not my problem."

The phone went dead.

3.

Martha sat hunched over the counter at the 7-Eleven, business was slow and she was bored.

She had been watching the flies hover over the lettuce for what seemed to be an hour. She couldn't understand why Mr. Visagie did not throw away old vegetables. He insisted on keeping everything till it turned brown and took on a new life in its ability to decompose and walk off by itself. The lettuce was an example of this: it had been in the shop for over a week now and was beginning to smell. Customers did not find this kind of thing appetising. But Mr. Visagie knew better, and would not listen to her, even though she was supposedly the assistant manager. Mr. Visagie was not a bad boss, he was actually a softie. His wife was the real businessperson and her transport business was thriving. Mr. Visagie ran the 7-Eleven so he could do something with his time, not that he did not work hard. Martha worked the one shift and he worked the other. He also employed a casual who mostly worked the day shift to help with offloading the deliveries. Andries was his name. He lived in the *township* just above the house where they lived. Sometimes he would catch up with her when she walked to work.

Martha had plenty of time to think about things when there were no customers. Foremost on her mind were the last twelve months, when the fortune of the family had turned. She could not believe that this time last year they still had a house, cars and a good reputation in the community of Welkom.

How could things change so quickly? Martha let out a huge sigh and felt the escaping breath on her hand.

Mr. Visagie waddled into the empty store, "Afternoon, afternoon, afternoon," he wheezed.

"Afternoon, Mr. Visagie," Martha respectfully greeted.

"Where are the customers today?" he enquired, raising his left eyebrow.

She smiled back as she had nothing to say to him.

"I have your wages with me. Would you like it now or at the end of your shift?"

"It's fine, Mr. Visagie, you can give it to me now," she said.

Mr. Visagie placed the burgundy briefcase he always carried with him on the counter. He fiddled with the combination, his podgy fingers unable to easily manoeuvre the combination keys, pulled the holders, opened the briefcase and then reached into it, all the while panting heavily. He noisily retrieved the envelopes inside and pulled out a bundle of paper, and placed it on the counter.

"I also have Hendrik and Magda's last payments from two months ago. I am going to give them all to you, if that is okay, unless they want to come in for them?"

"No, I will take them all, thank you." Martha said looking at him, but noticing that he could not make eye contact when he spoke about Hendrik or Magda. It was very nice of him to even offer them all jobs in the first place. He really was a kind Christian man to look after those that were less fortunate than himself. He had kept them all on as long as he could afford it, but the economy was not good in Wolseley. He had told her in the fourth month of their employment that he had no choice but to lay off two of them. But Martha knew that the real reason was because Hendrik was rude to the customers and Magda did not have any real experience. As she was the assistant manager, he had decided to keep her.

She also hoped that it had something to do with her looks. She might have been in her early fourties but she had nice skin and still had her figure from when she was younger. A figure that men still found attractive, she noticed when they noticed.

"I thought you had paid all the money?" she said.

"Well, I found that they had worked overtime on some days and I had not included it in the original wages," he explained, while closing the briefcase.

"Mr. Visagie, thank you."

"Not a problem, right then..." he said, muttering the rest of the sentence into the atmosphere as he waddled off to the office at the back of the store.

Martha carefully folded the envelopes and placed them in her handbag, which was hidden from view under the counter. She would count it later as she was only expecting her wages.

A local housewife walked in just as she was replacing her bag. "Morning, Madam," she said cheerfully. "Anything I can help you with?"

4.

Magda went into her bedroom and closed the door quietly behind her. She was scared. It looked like there were going to be more changes. She had had enough of change. First there was leaving Bothaville when Pa was retrenched because of this *BEE* thing, then the move to Welkom to where her uncle was, then the quick move to Wolseley because Ma knew a friend from there. Why couldn't they just stay somewhere for good?

She lay on her bed and switched on the radio. She liked to listen to Radio 5; she had listened to the station ever since she was a teenager. Her mother scolded her and told her that she should listen to an Afrikaans radio station and not to those Satanists that sang on the other stations. But she found comfort in this habit of hers. Not that this was her idea at all. When she was in high school in Welkom, her English friend Yolande Koekemoer said that listening to Radio 5 was cool and that only unsophisticated people listened to other radio stations. She had idolised Yolande with her beautiful blonde hair and her long eyelashes. She did not know why Yolande wanted to be her friend, she was so beautiful and Magda could not hide the fact that she was not a pretty girl. Yolande was the only friend Magda had made in Welkom.

When Magda looked into the mirror she hated what she saw looking back at her. Her mousy brown hair, always shapeless no matter what she did with it. Even when her mother bought her the hair crimper it had not helped, her hair refused to be shaped and not even thirty minutes after working it, it had returned back to its original state.

It was not her hair that was her greatest worry, Magda hated her mouth. Not just her mouth but what lay inside. Her teeth had grown all crooked and she was left with front teeth that stuck out at an unnatural degree. Her mother had promised her braces but as much as she pushed for them, there was always something else that needed the money more; the new television, or the gearbox of the car, which had packed up and which needed replacing. She could hear her mother now saying, "Money does not grow on trees but as soon as it does I will get you those braces, child."

She turned up the volume of the radio louder and then – realising that her father would scold her – plugged in her earphones and sunk into the latest song on the top 40 chart.

5.

"Bastard," he thought as the estate agent turned around and made his way out of the gate. Hendrik watched as he climbed into his car and drove off, leaving a cloud of dust behind him.

He had not expected to see Magda in the doorway of the house looking at him. She had witnessed the whole thing.

Both he and Martha had tried really hard to protect her from the world. From all of the things that happened which were negative. But sadly it was becoming more and more difficult. He also realised that by doing this should anything happen to either of them, she would not cope.

He had watched her become hysterical and after a brief exchange could not take it anymore and told her to go to her room and listen to the radio. It was a pleading, as well as a request, for him to have some time to think on his own.

Why was the Lord testing him in this manner? It was not for him to question but he wondered what more could be thrown his way? He was finding it more and more difficult to come back after each challenge.

His mind had thoughts racing through it but nothing logical came out of the mess inside.

He went through all the relatives he knew in his head, but again, like the last time this had happened, could not come up with any who would be able to help, or who were in a better position than himself. He could sell the *bakkie*, maybe some of their possessions, not that there was much left. Then what?

He found that he was pacing around the house, walking its perimeter again and again.

6.

Hendrik was mumbling. Why did more and more of what he was saying sound like shit? Martha looked at him and couldn't help feel that this was not what she had signed up for when marrying him. In each hand she had a plastic bag with groceries, which weighed on her shoulders, just like him. She put the plastic bags on the floor; sadly she couldn't do the same with him.

"We have to be out by the end of the month," he kept repeating, sitting lifeless on his favourite green chair, refusing to make eye contact.

"Did you explain to him that we need to get back on our feet?" she shot back, doubting even the simplest interactions with him.

"Yes, but he said that we had not paid for six months and the owner could not keep on like this."

"And did you explain that you and Magda have not been able to find jobs?" she asked accusingly.

"Yes...but...he didn't give me much time to speak to him before he left."

"I should have been here then at least I could have spoken to him properly," she said staring out of the window, not wanting to look at him.

"Are you saying that I didn't do my best?" he threw back, before she had even closed her mouth.

"Yes, I am. Do I have to do everything in this house, look after you and Magda, earn the money and then wipe your arse too?" she chided him.

"Stop before you go too far," the warning shot was fired.

"What do you mean? Far away from you and this bloody mess I find myself in?"

"Well then go," it was a threat that was used so often that it no longer had any effect.

"Maybe I will...Are you sure you tried to do something?"

"Of course I did, wife!" he spat back, visibly reddening around his neck as he now looked at her for the first time. "We would still have been in Welkom if it wasn't for you."

Martha had not expected that and she picked up the plastic bags with the groceries in them and walked out the lounge and into the kitchen.

She noisily unpacked them making sure to place each tin in the cupboard with maximum force. This was followed by her jerking open the fridge and then just as forcefully slamming it closed.

Bastard. Bastard…good for nothing, waste of oxygen bastard.

Martha had to control herself, or else she was going to go back into the lounge and hit him so hard, he would not breathe for a few days. She would make herself coffee and go and have a cigarette outside, somewhere where he could see her. Her secret stash of cigarettes for this exact occasion was well hidden in the kitchen cupboards. Hendrik was a man, and not a bright one at that. He did not go into the cupboards with the dry goods and so it was here that she hid her smokes and some cash that she had managed to hide from the family. Magda, like her father, never set foot in the kitchen other than to make toast for her breakfast or coffee for her father. While she took out her cigarettes she put the money that Mr. Visagie had wanted to give Hendrik with her secret stash. The bastard did not deserve it and she was not going to tell him about it. She would give Magda her money later, quietly.

Coffee making had never had such a ring, the kettle was filled with water that gushed out of the tap, the tin of Ricoffy was pulled out noisily and the teaspoon clanged on the side of it searching for the granules. The sugar bottle hit the counter as the sugar was exhumed and was violently stirred in the mug. Did he get the picture? Bastard.

She opened the back door and balancing her coffee, cigarette and lighter in one hand manoeuvred her way out of the house and into the garden. She sat on the stump at its far end so that he could see her smoking in full view. She made sure to place the cigarette in front of her at all times and to blow the smoke in the direction of the house. She felt calmer, stronger and back in control with each puff. She was going to teach this bastard a lesson if it were the last thing she did. No one was going to speak to her like that.

She put out the cigarette with the heel of her shoe, picked up the empty coffee cup and made her way back into the house.

She knew he had been watching, he could not help himself. Bastard.

7.

She heard the screaming even though the door was closed and the radio was on.

Sometimes her parents shouted at each other so badly that she thought one of them was going to kill the other. Once her Pa, in a rage, had taken an ashtray and thrown it so hard against the wall that the plaster had come away, exposing the raw brick underneath. The worst was when Ma had stomped around screaming at him, picking up things and slamming them down really hard, for emphasis, not for purposes of destruction. The glass coffee table was not meant to have that kind of treatment and it shattered when Ma picked up the ornament, the wooden statue of a man in a tuxedo kissing a woman that Pa had bought her for their anniversary, and slammed it down with a force to be reckoned with. They had all been in such shock, including Ma, that no one had spoken for the rest of the evening. Ma had swept up the glass and Pa locked himself in the spare bedroom.

The best thing to do at a time like this was to write a letter to Yolande. Although they no longer lived in the same town they still wrote to each other. When other friends were sending text messages or calling each other on cell phones, Yolande and Magda's preferred communication was by old-fashioned letter.

The real deal. Paper, envelopes, stamp, sealed with perfume (Yolande) and lip-gloss (Magda when it was available).

The truth was that Magda did not have a cell phone and so couldn't text or call. There was no extra money for that kind of luxury and Pa still had his cell phone from seven years ago. The battery did not work and the only way to use it was if it was plugged in. Pa no longer used it and sometimes her mother sent a *'Please call me'* to her uncle in Welkom and another friend somewhere, not that she really knew who it was, as her mother made the calls from her bedroom with the door closed.

Magda pulled out her little trunk where she stored her precious stationery. She and Yolande...Yolande and her would go once a week on a Saturday to the CNA or the stationery store in the mall to pick out a stationery set with writing paper and envelopes nicely packaged in a plastic sleeve. Yolande would always wrestle the set away from her and insist on paying for it. It was just the kind of person Yolande was. Her parents might have had money and she always spoilt Magda but never made her feel any less of a person. Afterwards they would go for a milkshake and chat about the latest movie stars or soap opera stars from their favourite shows, but they always had to be home to listen to the top 40 countdown on Radio 5.

She loved Yolande's house and she loved being spoilt by Yolande's mother. The Koekemoers had a reputation in the town as being different but were real pillars of the community. They were a little eccentric, Yolande's father who was Afrikaans had married her mother who was Scottish. The official language in the Koekemoer household was English and not Afrikaans. People always laughed when Mrs. Koekemoer spoke in her very funny accent in broken Afrikaans but never directly in front of her, except for younger children who did not know better. Mrs. Koekemoer therefore did not speak Afrikaans often, as she could sense the joke was on her.

The name Yolande is Afrikaans because she was named after Mr. Koekemoer's sister, who had died when she was a teenager, but Yolande's second name was Audrey – Yolande Audrey Koekemoer. Her mother's name was also Audrey; she made it clear that we could not call her *Tannie*, or Aunty Audrey.

"My name is Audrey," she said, as she flashed her perfect teeth. "Everyone calls me Audrey."

It was difficult at first to drop an old habit, to do something that no adult in the whole of Welkom would allow, but after a few corrections and some gentle nudging, Magda got it right, and started to call her 'Audrey,' like everyone else.

A visit to the Koekemoer's would start with tea and 'Audrey's' famous shortbread. It beat the rusks that Ma and Pa liked, as the shortbread was soft and melted in your mouth. 'Audrey' served tea, and not coffee, milky and sweet. As the chart show ran through lunch she also prepared the family traditional Saturday meal, which was not a *braai* but macaroni and cheese. 'Audrey' would not share the recipe with anyone. At twelve thirty there would be a knock and 'Audrey' would wheel in the trolley, set up the 'table,' a blanket on the floor, and present each girl with a steamy hot plate of noodles dripping with a creamy white sauce, with little pieces of bacon in it. The top of the macaroni was smothered in cheese and herbs, and grilled so that it went hard and crispy. Magda got used to this ritual very quickly, Saturdays were her favourite day, and she loved how special they made her feel. Yolande and her would then eat and chat in Afrikaans, and occasionally write down the line of a song they liked in their notebooks, never on the stationery they bought.

Magda was jolted out of her daydream by the noise coming from the kitchen. Ma was clearly angry about something.

She selected the butterfly paper set to write to Yolande on, because Yolande's last letter was on the paper with bows and they tried to use a different set to write back with.

Dear Yolande, she began her letter.

8.

Hendrik could feel the acid attack his stomach and the build-up rise through his mouth followed by the incredible burning sensation.

Hendrik had been told all his life that he asked too many questions. But surely this had to be a good thing and not a bad one? If you were not sure you had to ask questions. If you had the answers then there was a good chance that you were closer to understanding.

The first time he had ever been beaten was in the army when he was a reccy. He was beaten for asking questions. Questions that were logical and should have answers:

"What activity had these men been up to?"

"What was required to be done?"

"What exactly did disappear mean?"

"Literally make them disappear?"

"Kill them?"

Two days later, when he woke up in a military hospital, he vaguely remembered the force of the butt of a gun against his head, near his temple. When he asked what had happened no one could answer the question.

He was a good man; he had been a good husband for as long as he could, he had provided when he had the means. Being white had changed. Before, he could guarantee a stable life for his family, now it was a joke. Reverse racism, and if he could go back he would hit F.W. De Klerk so hard that the man would never have given the land back to the communists. The communists he had been told to keep at bay. Now it was rubbed in his face every day of his life - "comrade this," "comrade that," money wasted on extravagance - while he could not even support his family anymore.

He had given his youth for this country and what had he got in return? Nothing, absolutely nothing.

When he prayed in the morning and evening, he asked God these questions. He wanted answers. He didn't challenge God, it was not his place, but some kind of explanation would have helped him. He could feel himself fading into the dark, into a place where he was going to take his life because he no longer had control.

He had to stop thinking like this, he told himself.

His whole body was hot, overheated by the exchange with Martha. He had never treated her in any way like she had just done him. She should be the one behaving, apologising. She had forgotten quickly.

He tried to think about other things, like if this were his house he could at least do something about the garden, or do something to maintain it, but it wasn't. Some days he paced around the house, many times, trying to imagine what he would do. Scrape the walls, then paint them. Plant something in the garden. Vegetables, there was no doubt that he came from farming stock. Good farming stock at that. His father had farmed in the Free State in Senekal until his brother had mismanaged the farm, sending his birthright into the hands of a liquidator. He was too young to understand what was happening. He knew that they moved to the town and that his brother then moved to Welkom.

Pointless, pointless, pointless thoughts, he chided himself.

"Hmmarrgh," he noticed the sound he had made and was startled that it had come from his person. It was the thing that brought him back to reality, back into his body.

9.

Martha closed the door and plugged in the phone. Hendrik's idea was just stupid, not even stupid, actually ridiculous. Selling their last remaining possessions would not raise enough money to pay back the rent. Even if it did, all it would do is settle up the debt and they would have nothing over. Hendrik was not thinking about the long-term plan as usual. Had that estate agent not explained that the house had been sold? What was the point of selling their stuff if they could not stay here any longer?

They really had no savings left. Each incident depleted them more and now they lived from pay-cheque to pay-cheque, in this case Martha's pay-cheque. Her money that she had been secretly saving was enough for a little emergency, but not for bailing them out of a crisis. If she told Hendrik about it she was sure he would have given it to the estate agent – he was unable to understand that once you are in this far there is no turning back.

She sent the *'Please call me'* and sat down on the bed to wait. Sometimes his phone was off, or he left it somewhere and didn't hear the text message come through. Luckily after less than a minute the phone rang.

"Hello," she said.

"I miss you," the voice on the other side said, without returning the greeting.

"You, too," she responded flatly.

"The divorce is final," he said. "Last week it was all wrapped up."

"I thought she wanted to forgive you?"

"So did I, but..."

"What is happening with the house and the kids?"

"I gave it to her, with some money. The children don't talk to me anyway."

"I see."

"I have bought a flat in town and have moved my stuff there."

"Good for you."

"I miss you."

"You said that already." She started to cry, the tears travelling down the sides of her face, weaving down her cheeks and landing on the mobile phone.

"What's wrong?"

"Things are not good here."

"Why? Tell me?" the voice was more frantic. "Martha, you have to tell me what is going on?"

The floodgates were open now and the sobbing took over her body. She had no more control. Her body went into convulsions with each uncontrollable sob, followed by a stream of tears. She pushed the red button on the phone, unplugged it from the plug, lay down on the bed and continued to cry.

Eventually the tears subsided and she lay on the bed motionless, unable to move. She looked into the naked light bulb on her side table. She could stare at the lit light bulb for ages. When it was too painful to look at it any longer she blinked, and blinked and blinked, seeing the light in her vision again and again and again.

10.

Magda didn't know what she should do. Pa had told her to collect all the things they did not use and place them in the unused bedroom so that they could sell them. Ma had said that it was pointless, rebuking Pa and then they had screamed at each other and she had closed her bedroom door.

Magda didn't want to tell them that she was scared and unsure. She did not like this feeling. She also wanted to talk to someone about her insecurities, but there was no one. This was not something that she could tell Yolande. Although Yolande was her best friend in the whole world, this matter, the situation, was something that they could not easily converse about. She was also scared that if she got too serious in the letters Yolande might not write back. That was something that she looked forward to each week and could not afford to compromise.

Yolande's letter was normally delivered on a Thursday and she would wait patiently for it. She knew the postman, Andile, and sat on the front verandah from two in the afternoon to greet him, as this was the last stop on his round.

Ma and Pa had been like this since they moved to Welkom. Pa would shout and Ma would shout right back. Magda always took cover in her room. She would quietly creep into it as soon as the voices started to get louder. Later, when they moved here to Wolseley, they no longer spoke to each other anyway. She could not remember the last time they had actually had a conversation and not a fight.

She missed the family meals that they used to eat together, with some conversation and a joke or some teasing about something.

Pa had lost his appetite after Welkom and sometimes he didn't even eat. Ma ate in the kitchen by herself; sometimes she ate while she cooked. She also did not eat that much.

Ma also no longer made the really nice dishes like *waterblommetjiebredie* or her oxtail stew that Pa loved so much. Meals were now omelettes or tin food.

They had eaten together in Welkom last before the incident with the glass coffee table. After that meals were dished up and left in the kitchen. You could eat your meal anywhere you wanted. It was clear that Ma and Pa were not going to eat together and so she brought her own food to her room and spread out her blanket on the floor and had a picnic with herself, just like she and Yolande used to do.

11.

Hendrik had developed a terrible pain under his rib. It burned, but when he poked there, a sharp shooting pain responded to his touch. The more he fought with Martha, the more the pain intensified.

Even his body was giving in now. This life of his had become unbearable. He wanted to go out into the bush, out into his beloved Africa, where as a child he played with his friends, where the land was the source of their entertainment. He longed to breathe in the air and smell the savannah.

Every happy memory in his life was based somewhere in the *veld*, like his army tracking days when they followed people over the mountains between South Africa and Swaziland. Not leaving behind any trails, no evidence, like ghosts moving through the night. And no matter how hard they tried to run away they inevitably found their prey. The bush hid so many secrets that were too cruel to contemplate. He was doing his duty, he was following orders and that was one thing that he was very good at.

But he didn't want to think of that now, he didn't want to remember the past because then he was forced to acknowledge that it was somehow wrong.

His favourite memory in the whole world, the one that was his heaven, the one that no one could take away, that was the one he wanted to remember now:

Martha, the sun, walking through the open *veld* with a picnic basket, packed with sandwiches they had made, and a flask of coffee.

Spreading out the blanket on the piece of rock that overlooked the valley below, he said to her, "You are the most beautiful woman in the world." And at that moment he felt it. It was the first time in his life that he forgot to breathe and had to restart his breathing manually. She had been embarrassed by the statement; however, his intention was not to flatter, but rather to tell her how he felt at that moment.

She looked down and her eyelashes were caught by the sun, it was then that he noticed how long and delicate they were.

The kiss was a natural transition. Her lips like two butterfly pupae, the adults underneath, ready to come out. When their lips touched and her mouth opened he tasted the butterflies take flight. Although he was a man and men were supposed to be strong, a tear had welled up in his eye and he had brushed it away before Martha could notice.

That was all that happened: one beautiful, soft kiss loaded with so much beauty that, thinking back on it, he could stop time. He could replay the moment, and no matter what the distraction, it helped him to put things in perspective.

He could not understand that even when he fought with Martha that this memory still had the power to overcome his anger. Did this mean that the Martha now was not the same as the person that he knew in the past?

He had an aunt who was convinced that a soul could leave a body and be replaced by another. She was so convinced by this she would always tell the story about her friend Hettie, who was a busybody, with so much energy and who knew everyone's business in their town and the next. Hettie could bake, sew and chatter all at the same time. Then, overnight, she went quiet. She stopped taking an interest in the very things that she had thrived on. People would come to *skinner* and she would walk out midway through their conversations.

She did not even want to organise the church fête, something that she had commandeered for over thirty years. "Just like that!" his aunt would say and then clap her hands together for extra emphasis. Her soul had walked right out of her body. It had decided that was enough and just disappeared into the atmosphere. What replaced it was another soul, another person, another Hettie or another person called Wilma.

This is the only explanation of what could have happened to Martha. The person who screamed at him was not the same person who had touched the top of the grass as she walked, who had stopped every now and then to smell a wildflower, even though she would say that they had no smell, the same person who would look up and say, "It is good to be alive here in God's Eden."

The rage, the face, the onslaught - all of that was another soul - that was Wilma.

12.

Martha was smoking in the bedroom. She did not care anymore. She was tired of fighting. Hendrik did not even have the masculinity to fight back. He didn't deserve even the partial respect of her smoking outside.

What the hell was there to sell? There was nothing left anyway. When they had left Welkom all of the contents that they brought fitted into one PX container box. They had left behind most of what one collected in a life: the ornaments, the toaster that did not work but could not be thrown out.

So now what? She already knew the answer to the question. There was nothing left. As a family they had used up all of the options.

She plugged in the phone. *'Please call me'*.

She waited. The phone did not ring. It did not ring for the next hour either. She was about to unplug it when the ringing sound cut through the silence.

"Hello."

"Hello."

"Martha, I have been so worried about you. Please, this is eating at me."

"I am sorry, I couldn't talk to you. I had to stop."

"Martha, must I come and fetch you?"

"You know that is not possible." Her voice broke for a split second. Not today, she needed to talk reality and she needed to talk it with someone.

"Are you okay?"

"No. I am not okay, but I can't talk about me anymore. What becomes of people like us?"

"The three of you have no hope, it is not what you want to hear, but you know it."

"Yes, I know it."

"What does Hendrik say?"

"That we should drive to Cape Town, try and find work there, get back on our feet."

"Where would you stay?"

"I have no idea."

"There has got to be something else."

"You said that there was no hope."

"So Cape Town is the last chance?"

"I don't want to make a decision and nor does Hendrik. It is so final, whatever that decision is."

"You still have the job, don't you?"

"Yes, but it only pays a few thousand. It doesn't even cover the rent, my whole salary."

"You still have some income though. Is it not better to stay there?"

"At least if we go to Cape Town there is a chance that we could all get work."

"And if no one gets work?"

"I can't think about that. This is what we need to do."

"Now it is we?"

"Stop, please."

"I could deposit some money, I don't have much each month after the divorce, but I could make a plan."

"No..."

"Forget your pride."

"Don't worry, I have no pride left."

"Then what is it?"

"I wish Hendrik would die."

"Martha, that is strong, even for you."

"No, really, he is like a wet blanket that has been placed over my head that I am struggling to throw off but can't."

"Martha, please."

"I have to go," without saying good-bye, she hangs up and quickly pulls the plug from the socket.

There, it was out. She actually said it aloud. It terrified her.

What would it be to place a pillow over his head while he was sleeping?

Sometimes God was cruel.

13.

Ma had made coffee and her some tea and suggests that they talk about a few things.

"Close the door, Magda."

She never closes her door; it seems almost strange, unnatural. The door does not close fully. She has never tried to close it before so she has not noticed that the door does not fit into the frame. From behind her she hears, "That is fine, come sit here next to me."

Magda has a small single bed in her room. She sits alongside her mother as she cannot sit across from her.

"We have to talk about what is happening."

Magda does not know how to respond to this, and says nothing.

"Things are not good, Magda."

She wants to answer but no words come out.

"There are not many options left, my child." Her mother awkwardly takes a sip from the coffee cup she is holding. Magda listens to her mother as she swallows. She then sighs out lightly and continues, "You need to prepare yourself."

"Um…for what, Ma? What should I prepare myself for?"

"Well, for, well for um…what is about to happen."

Ma didn't make sense to her. She couldn't get what Ma was trying to say. She waited for Ma to say more, but instead an awkward silence followed. After what seemed like an hour Ma stood up, took her cup and picked up Magda's untouched tea and quietly walked out.

Magda's eyes followed her as she left, looking for any possible clue but there was nothing more.

14.

"Jesus loves me, this I know, for the bible tells me so," Hendrik sings quietly to himself. He has been calling on God to intervene in his life but so far there are only ten days to go until they need to leave the house. They need a miracle, before it's too late.

He mulled Martha's solution over and over in his head and could not see how it would be possible, how they could live in a *bakkie* while they all looked for work in Cape Town. At least the money Martha earned now fed Magda and herself, what if that was gone as well? Hendrik didn't like gambling and this felt to him like they were going to make a decision in which they were going to lose everything. They had so little left, what if they lost even that, then what?

"Lord, please guide us, please," he mumbles quietly, "please Lord, please."

At least the Lord had intervened with Martha: she had stopped shouting at him. She did not speak much, but at least she did not fly into a rage just at the sight of him.

"Thank you, Lord," he mutters and he notices that he is drooling. Saliva has dripped onto his shirt. His hands are working in slow motion and he struggles to get his fingers to the wet patch. Even when his fingers have managed to get there, he is unable to get them to co-operate and mop up the mess. He tries to call out to Magda and observes as a strange, muffled sound escapes his closed mouth.

He closes his eyes to try and stop panicking; maybe he is having a stroke. Oh please God take me, he thinks. I am no more use here. Nothing else happens. He is still awake, still in the same place. He is not dead. He tries to squeeze his eyes even tighter but cannot manage to do that. He must focus on other things; he must recall the last conversation with Martha.

"Hendrik," she looks him directly in the eye. It is the first time in a year that she does this, "I have not come here to fight with you." It is a statement, not a plea.

"We don't have many options left. It is time to think about what we should do next."

He feels he has been hypnotised as she speaks to him. He does not respond, he does not interact, he is under the spell of her voice. She continues to speak.

"I think we should all go to Cape Town."

He continues to stare.

"It does not make sense for us to stay in Wolseley," she looks around as if she can see out of the walls and down the streets of the town. Travelling past the 7-Eleven with her eyes and down the main road, scorning the town that has been home to them.

"In Cape Town we all stand a chance of getting work." The proposal laid out before him. "If all of us work we can rebuild our family." He remembers this part of the speech from another time. It was what she had said when she had decided the family should move to Wolseley.

He snapped out of it. "We don't have anywhere to stay in Cape Town."

She sighs, sensing the stirrings of resistance.

"What else do we do, Hendrik?" she looked at him not with hatred but pity.

It is now his turn to sigh.

"Hendrik, we can sleep in the *bakkie* until we have saved up enough for rent. We can rent a *maid's* quarters or small flat and share until we can afford something better."

The words bounced about and he could not make sense of what she was saying. She carried on talking but he couldn't understand.

She was gone a minute or two later and he was alone again in the green chair. The only remaining chair in the house.

"The Lord is my shepherd, I shall not want…"

He is silent and even his inner voice is too. He can feel the heat pulsing through his body and his feet, then arms, then fingers. His eyes unlock and he can open them.

He is alive.

15.

Martha stands in the doorway looking at the collection of things on the floor. It is a pitiful sight. They don't have much to begin with and all the contents of their life, the leftovers, not many will want.

Hendrik had thought she was opposed to the idea of the sale, but she was not. It would make things easier in her mind. Could they not just dump the stuff up the road at the *'location'* rather than go through the humiliation of the sale? Someone had to officiate whilst people browsed through your stuff. They would make decisions about whether to take it or not and judge you on something that had been a part of your life.

On the floor, next to a broken toaster and the *snackwich* machine, lay the clock that Hendriks' mother had given them when they got engaged. She had said that time would continue like their marriage, forever. Martha bent over and stared at the clock. It had stopped working more than ten years ago. She had not expected to see that lying here. Was she upset? She wasn't sure of her feelings; they were intertwined with reason. She had prepared herself to sell her car when they could no longer afford it. She had also sold her independence, as she had liked to drive whenever she wanted to think, not far away, but around the outskirts of town. She had saved to buy the car and when she had sold it, it was already 12 years old. It had to be done. They only needed one car; they could only afford one car.

When she had to sell her jewellery that was when she had started to sell pieces of herself. First her watch, then her bangles, then the necklace with the small diamond, but along with it went her heart. Hendrik had bought it the first year that they had celebrated their anniversary. She had secretly cried outside the pawnshop, not because of Hendrik but because it reminded her of herself, what it was that identified her as a person. After that, it was easy to sell the rings except for the engagement ring with its diamond, which she would admire for the way that it caught the light and fractured beauty. Hendrik did not have anything to sell. He did not own any jewellery. His wedding band was the only thing he wore. How could he know what it feels like then, to sell yourself? He owned, and was nothing of value. He had no hobbies, no taste for anything. The more she thought about it, the more she realised that he was content with very little. He never made demands of how money was to be spent. He handed his salary to her when he was originally paid in cash, when later he was paid through a cheque and then even later when paid through a bank account, he had even given Martha's bank account number. When he wanted to buy her something like jewellery they would go to American Swiss and pick out what she wanted and then she would pay with his money. Could she say he lived through her?

16.

Magda looks around the room. The bed is now gone, as is the small table. On the floor is the place she has slept for the past three days. Two cushions have been crudely lined up to form something of a bed, but there is really only the pink duvet with the bunnies on it left. Ma had lectured her when she had lost her temper. The words had lingered in the shell of the house ever since.

"No point fighting this, my girl. Welcome to reality. The sooner you accept this, the sooner you can move on with your life."

She had stopped writing letters to Yolande, as this didn't seem to matter anymore. Nothing seemed to matter anymore. She had never been so scared in all her life; and the realisation of what lay ahead had started to resonate with her.

Ma had made it clear that everything that was not sold was staying behind; there was nowhere to store it. This wasn't true because she could have asked to store it in the storeroom at the back of the 7-Eleven. It was basically wasted space and empty.

There is still too much in the house to leave behind. She was surprised that so much had sold on the day of the garage sale. Even in the current situation, people liked to buy impulsively and Ma had re-priced everything to nearly nothing. People could smell the bargain, and some the desperation, and further negotiated lower prices.

Pa had hid in the house complaining of a cold, but she knew he was hiding in the house because of shame, not illness. Ma had handled everything, working like a robot, issuing orders to Magda of what to pack and for whom.

The lawn was littered with a few small articles at the end, which Ma then gave to people for an all-inclusive price. Ma had shown no emotion and made no small talk. She was even finished before twelve so that she could start her shift at the 7-Eleven on time.

Magda picked up the last remaining pieces and carried them into the now empty house. Pa pretended to be asleep, but she could hear him breathing normally.

Three days of confusion, quiet and emptiness later, and here she was staring yet again into the bareness of her room.

Ma had said one bag each, there would not be much space to begin with, but once they were settled in Cape Town, then they would be able to start over. This was proving to be more difficult than she had initially thought: what could be replaced and not? As the afternoon wore on she had packed and repacked her gym bag ten times, each time hoping that this time all the things she wanted to take would fit in, but that was never the case. Out of sheer frustration she abandoned the task and quietly let herself out the back door, not that her father had spoken in the last three days, but she preferred not to bother him.

She looked around the space at the back of the house: the wild grass that grew over the area and the stable which her mother smoked in.

They had not been here long and she had never felt connected to the town. She had no friends, she smiled at some people when working at the 7-Eleven, but these were not even acquaintances, just people from the town.

She started to cry. A quiet sadness.

17.

Please Lord, take my life so that I don't have to, he pleaded again, and again, but was still alive and he had offered up this prayer for weeks on end.

When he still had money to buy the *Beeld* on a Sunday he remembered being shocked by the stories of fathers who had shot their families and then themselves. He remembered quite clearly that judgement, as well as the recurring thought 'it could never get that bad.'

How could it be planned? When conscious thought had to be utilised, which required the processing of ideas. Selecting the time, date and who to shoot first. The logistics of getting your family into one room. Did they say anything to their family before shooting? Logic said no, because this implied that there had to be a thought process behind it – a plan. Surely no one could go completely through this kind of action with any logic or planning.

But it was not this thought that worried him the most. He imagined his wife and daughter in front of him. The eyes, eyebrows, nose and lips of his daughter. The mole that lay between the bottom of her cheek and the start of her mouth. Something which only belonged to her. Her unique marking.

How could he kill the very thing that he had created? There was no way he could shoot her if he had to see her face before him. Back to planning. If he were not going to see her face, he could not make any noise and that would require planning.

How weird did the planning seem, but he now realised the need for it.

He knew his wife did not love him anymore. Welkom had taught him that. Did he hate her for it? No, he was disappointed at his failure to be a man.

Her face at their wedding would be the reminder point. That porcelain face, brimming with happiness as they swirled around the church hall to that *Dirty Dancing* song. With each turn she beamed and at the end the kiss on his lips, initiated by her. It had tasted completely different to any he had had before, or after. He felt foolish thinking it tasted like liquid strawberry, but it did.

How could he pick up a gun; go through the act of loading the bullet, placing it inside the gun; raising it so that it was in line with her head; aiming carefully to minimise the damage and the need for a second bullet; pulling the trigger - actively sending a message to one finger to squeeze? All of this required thought. All of this required planning. It involved decisions.

No, he had changed his mind. He did not judge those people who took their families' lives, because it required effort and planning, and he, Hendrik, was too much of a coward for that.

'Our Father who art in heaven, hallowed be your name, thy kingdom come, thy will be done on earth as it is in heaven.'

18.

Martha left the *bakkie* at home. She didn't want to see Hendrik, and although she did not need permission to take the vehicle, the keys were in the lounge and that meant interaction with him that, in turn, required energy.

Ever since that fateful day of the garage sale she did not want to even know he existed. What a waste of a human being! The tragedy of marriage, a child and responsibility was slowly suffocating the very air out of her.

She was tired of being the accountable one, the problem solver.

The irony of Welkom – she would have had a job and place to stay - he would not have. Having to leave because of her was his way of trying to protect whatever dignity was left. No, Welkom did not require her to place the scarlet A on her clothes and parade around town like the latest whore who opened shop outside the church. Her hatred for Hendrik was intense, but her need to protect his dignity overcame that. If she was looking for blame it was her Afrikaner Calvinist roots.

Wolseley became the afterthought, the beacon of hope for Hendrik, but he was weak and pathetic, reduced to the state of a child who needed a mother and protector. The two children, her child and her husband-child, consumed her, eating at every last piece of energy she had.

She had crossed over the bridge into town and stopped and looked at what had become of her life. She would never have thought this in a million years. A town lost in time and space, a life burning up around her, no money, no possessions, no future. She stopped walking as she felt her balance go and grabbed the side of the bridge to steady herself.

The next few days were not going to be easy and the ones after that even more uncertain. She needed to focus on today, on now, or it would overwhelm her.

Without thinking, her hand reaches for the pocket where her cigarettes are kept. One is alight in her hand and she is already breathing out smoke when she realises that she is smoking. Smoking on a bridge to nowhere.

19.

Magda is trying to comprehend what she has just heard. The words and the thought and the way her mother said it all don't make sense. She feels again like a little girl, forced to make adult decisions.

"Magda, I want you to think about what I just said," her mother says, not angry or irritated.

"Sorry, Ma," she hears herself say, "please can you explain it again."

Instead of speaking immediately her mother walks to the end of her bedroom, where her small desk used to be. Supporting her back against the wall she gently eases herself into a sitting position on the floor. She motions for Magda to come over and sit next to her.

Why was her mother acting so weirdly she thought? What was she trying to achieve?

She knows better than not to follow instructions and finds herself joining her mother for the meeting on the floor. She looks at her mother's face which is too close, and sees the lines that have been carved into it, the lines that represent the last few years. But now there are also dark rings underneath her eyes. These rings have taken her eyes and sunk them deep into her skull. Her mother has taken strain.

"Magda, I have spoken to your uncle," she starts, but then stops just as suddenly. The silence is uncomfortable and she leans forward and touches her mother's knee. The action doesn't break the silence or get the response she is hoping for. Nothing happens.

"Yes, Ma, you spoke to uncle," she repeats to show she is listening and is awaiting more information.

It must be the action of talking that brings her mother back to life, for she looks for the first time straight into her eyes, with the force of her full gaze. Magda is scared because what she sees is her mother unguarded, vulnerable and scared.

"Magda," she begins again, "what I am about to tell you, you must promise and swear by Jesus, that you will not tell your father."

Her mother's eyes pierce her and she feels herself falling under a trance.

"Magda, I said you must swear on Jesus. Now swear on Jesus that you will not tell your father," her voice rising in pitch.

Magda feels torn between what her mother wants and what she was taught in Sunday school, where you never swear on the life of Jesus. Not wanting to upset her mother more than she already is, she looks down and utters, "Ma, I can't swear on the Lord Jesus, that is what I was taught, it is wrong and I can go to hell."

Her mother lets out a deep breath exhaling slowly not in anger but contemplation. When all the air has been expelled from her lungs, she again looks at Magda in the eye, "Thank you, my child, for saying that. You are right, we are not just allowed to use the Lord's name when we like." Inhale new oxygen into the lungs. "I am trying to show you how serious this is, how much I need to speak to you about it, how much I need you to then promise me that you will never tell your father, never, ever, ever."

Magda now feels like she does not have enough breath and inhales deeply, too.

"Ma, I promise," she says but her eyes betray her because she can no longer look her mother in the eye.

"Magda, if you want to tell your father that is your choice, but know that I, your mother, asked you not to."

Magda can feel her cheeks on fire as the shame of her actions becomes evident in the innocence of her body.

"Ma, you can trust me."

"Thank you, Magda."

Her mother reaches over and cups her hands in hers, silence again, but it is a different silence this time, because it remains that way for many minutes but Magda feels okay with it.

When her mother is ready she releases Magda's hand.

"I spoke to your uncle and he said that we can come back to Welkom, but without your father."

Before her mother is even finished the word she snaps, "But Ma, how can we?" Her mother is not making sense because it sounds to her as if she wants to go back to Welkom without her father.

"Magda, he does not have space for all of us."

"But, Ma," she reasons, "what would happen to Pa?"

"It is called life, my child," her voice wavers when she says this. "I have to think of you."

"But Ma, how can we wake up in the morning, knowing that Pa is somewhere...we don't even know where he is?"

"Magda, don't you think I haven't thought of this before? I am not a bad person, but, my child, those are your uncle's terms."

"Well, Ma, I can't be without Pa and Pa can't be without us. He needs us."

"I am not asking you to make up your mind now but we have to leave this house in five days and then there is no going back."

Her insides have gone lame and she feels like she is drowning, not to mention, her heart is racing. Is this how Anne Frank felt she thinks, when trying to claw onto any normalcy? Trapped but wanting to escape.

Her mother breaks her panic, "Magda, what if you and only you, went to Welkom?"

This does not ease her panic and the torrent of tears takes hold and she starts to shake violently. Even shielded within the familiar embrace of her mother, she no longer feels secure.

20.

The phone is having difficulty connecting. She dials and receives a funny signal and then has to dial again. After many attempts, she slams it against the wall. The phone is so old and bulky that it bounces off, not showing any signs of damage.

She lights a cigarette, breathing in the nicotine until she feels the usual comfort that this brings. Hendrik no longer sleeps in the bedroom, since the fateful garage sale day, and even if they were sharing the same space now she would have lit up as a way to chastise him.

She hangs the cigarette in her mouth while she replaces the elastic band that holds the charger together. She plugs the charger back into the wall and retrieves the cigarette with her fingers, a plume of smoke swirls about her.

Once the phone powers up she gives the number another try; this time it connects with minimal effort. She lets it ring three times and then hangs up. Within a few seconds her phone rings.

"How are you?" he asks, with what sounds like genuine concern.

"Hi. I'm as good as I can be."

"Did you get the money I deposited into your account?"

"I said you didn't need to, but thank you. You shouldn't have."

"What are your plans?"

"I spoke to Magda."

"And..."

"She said she couldn't leave her father."

"So..."

"I don't know..."

"Not good."

"I..."

"Yes."

"I have to go...sorry." She hangs up before he can say anymore.

The cigarette is lifeless in her left hand and she flicks it watching the ash snow onto the bare floor below.

21.

They haven't even noticed that he has not eaten anything in two days. Not that meals are prepared or distributed, as in the past.

Please Lord, let me die.

Please Lord, let me die.

Please Lord, I have never asked for much. Please let me die.

Silence.

'Our father who art in heaven, by they name kingdom come, hallowing hallow hello.'

22.

Ma says she will ask to use the storeroom at the 7-Eleven. Magda feels the first sign of hope since that fateful day with the estate agent. When her mother mentions this, the tears just fell and her mother had hugged her and told her the Lord would look after them and everything would be okay.

Although she had finally made a decision about what would go in the gym bag with her to Cape Town, she could now at least leave behind her nice stationery and her photographs as these would be locked in the storeroom.

But there was that conversation she had been part of. The one requesting they leave for Welkom without her father that would not go away. Her mother's face, the statement, her mother's face, a question, her mother's hands.

This event had forced her to think about her father, something that she had not done for a long time. Her father, the beacon, her father, a voice of authority, her father, who had carried her into the waves at the seaside. How could Ma have even asked her to think of leaving him? And not just leave him, but leave him behind, like her photographs in the storeroom at the 7-Eleven.

After her mother leaves for work Magda quietly walks into the lounge and peers at the floor on which her father lies curled up into a ball. He is sleeping and small sounds expel from his lips.

"Pa," she calls, "Pa."

He stirs and opens his eyes.

"Pa, is there anything I can get you?"

He unbundles himself and looks at her baffled.

"Coffee, Pa? Would you like some nice coffee?"

She doesn't wait to hear his response but walks to the kitchen and boils the kettle. Soon she is busy making a cup of coffee for her father.

She hands the steaming mug to him and he reaches for it with both hands.

"Thank you, my child, that is very kind of you." His hands continue to shake but he takes a sip, looks at her again and says, "This is the nicest cup of coffee."

"Ma says she will ask Mr. Visagie to use the storeroom."

"That will be very helpful."

"Has Pa decided what you are going to take in your bag to Cape Town?" she asks.

"Not yet."

"Maybe I can help you, Pa?"

"That sounds good, then we can plan what to take to the storeroom."

"Yes, Pa, and then maybe you can help me too."

He touches her arm and says quietly, "Thank you."

She takes the now empty cup from his other hand and reaches over and kisses him on the cheek.

While she is in the kitchen she remembers back to a time when she would kiss his cheek in the morning before he went to work 'for good luck,' and then again when he came back home, 'because he had been lucky.' That time is now past.

23.

He feels himself coming out of the dark tunnel. He is such a simple being.

The Lord is teaching him a lesson, an important one. He has a family and he must do something, even if it is to help Magda decide what to pack.

He must get his focus back so that he can drive the *bakkie* the one and a half hours to Cape Town, not that he has ever made the journey and assumes it is that long. The road, the cargo, two family members and three bags. Bedding to sleep in the back of the *bakkie*. That reminds him, the canopy lock needs to be checked.

Suddenly there is so much to do. Can one cup of coffee have this effect, or the magic of his child?

He not only needs to plan his bag but he needs to find a place to store the remainder of the goods. Martha would not ask her boss, but he would. All they needed was a bit of help.

24.

She cannot believe that he went behind her back to ask if they could use the storeroom at the 7-Eleven. From lifeless to wanting to offer help, Bastard.

She never wanted to put Mr. Visagie in that position, one where you look at the desperation in front of you and concede to things you wouldn't normally do, just because you were made to feel sorry.

Bastard.

When Mr. Visagie had mentioned it to her she must have registered shock, because he stopped talking and just looked at her. It was like something from one of those slapstick movies. His face was comic and half-opened. If this were a comedy some drool would have dribbled from his mouth. But this was life, so there was nothing but 'the look.'

"Sorry," she said, clearly irritated, "I am so sorry he asked you."

"Not to worry, really…"

"He did not speak to me about it. I will speak to him at the end of my shift."

"Please use it." He walks away at this point and she cannot say anymore.

Martha is so angry at this revelation that she serves the few customers that visit with cold precision. She counts the minutes down to when she can go and smack him, because today she was going to cross that line.

When her shift does come to an end she gets into the *bakkie* and drives home recklessly through stop streets, hooting at pedestrians.

Almost before she has even pulled the handbrake up, she opens the car door and moves to the front of the house.

She struggles to get the key into the lock and fights to open the door. She has never had problems opening this door, but today it must be like this.

After much shaking the door opens, it is Magda.

"Hello, Ma, is there a problem with your key?"

"*Blerrie* key won't open the door. Sorry, my child," she roars, "swearing is bad."

Her daughter hugs her and squeezes her close. She is caught off guard and stands still, allowing the hug.

Magda whispers to her, "Pa and I are preparing our bags and sorting out what needs to go with us." Before she can say anything she catches the eye of Hendrik, sitting on the floor cross-legged looking at her, but there is no judgment in his eyes. His eyes tell her everything; he must have heard from Magda about the storeroom. He must also have known that she was not going to really ask.

The man looking up at her is not the pitiful man who has been resident, but not present, in her life. It is a man who is very much alive. She hasn't seen this man in years, it is no wonder she feels disoriented.

"Sorry, it has been a long day," she says, untangling herself from her daughter's hold, she feels claustrophobic. "I have a bad headache. I am going to lie down for a few minutes."

She does not turn the light on in the bedroom but goes to lie on the floor. She looks up into the darkness of the roof and beyond and closes her eyes.

25.

Although there is too much stuff for one bag, what eventually goes to the storeroom easily fits onto the back of the *bakkie.*

Magda helps her father load the *bakkie*; it feels like it takes the whole morning but it only takes an hour.

Pa insists that they clean the house before they give the keys back to the estate agent. In his words, "There is a right way of doing things."

They had come to Wolseley with very little but were leaving with nothing but the clothes on their back. Magda had stopped processing this since her father started to get things done. But now, looking again over the contents of the back of the *bakkie,* that sinking feeling in the bottom of her stomach reared its ugly head.

"Pa," she asks, "everything will be okay, Pa? Won't it?"

There is no answer from the front of the *bakkie* into which her father was packing some newspapers that they hadn't used. Knowing him, he wanted them recycled at the 7-Eleven.

"Pa," she calls this time louder and her father's hand appears from behind the door.

"Yes, my girl?"

She looks at his face; a face filled with so much resolve and says, "Is there anything else I can help you with?"

"No, my child. Nearly ready to take this to the 7-Eleven and fetch your mother."

"Okay, Pa."

She hooks the back of the *bakkie* closed and checks to make sure everything is secured. The door locks without any problems and she joins her father in the front of the *bakkie*.

They are about to make their way to the store with the remainder of their belongings. It is then that she remembers that her mother washed her 7-Eleven shirt and asked Magda to iron it and take it with.

"Sorry, Pa. I forgot to take Ma's shirt."

She unlocks the door and retrieves the plastic bag from the kitchen. The sounds of her footsteps echo as she walks back to the front door.

26.

Hendrik parks the *bakkie* behind the 7-Eleven next to the storage room.

"Magda, my girl, go and get the key from your mother."

"Yes, Pa," she replies and disappears round to the front side of the store.

He opens the back up and slowly starts to unload. He neatly packs the boxes and remaining household items in a row next to the storeroom door. He has already unpacked the *bakkie*, as well as the newspapers from the front but Magda has not come back with the key. They are probably trying to find it, as the room is never used, well not while he worked there.

Hendrik now starts to think about Cape Town and what needs to be done. He is sure he will be able to get a job, any job, and work himself up from there. All he needed was some opportunity and Cape Town was big and hopefully full of it. He was sure it was not going to be an easy ride, but things would sort themselves out.

Still no Magda. Hendrik looks at his watch, there is time, as the estate agent is coming to collect the keys only at four. He is a little bit irritated but time is the one thing they will now have plenty of.

Magda brings him out of his thoughts. "Sorry Pa, Mr. Visagie and Ma are not there and Mrs. Visagie did not know anything about us using the storeroom. Mrs. Visagie tried to call Mr. Visagie but he did not answer his phone. Then Mrs. Visagie had to look for the key."

He was worried now because he did not want to get Mr. Visagie into trouble.

"Pa, I asked her and she understands, and she found the key. Here it is." She displays the key for him to see.

He is still worried about the imposition on the Visagies, which is now evident.

Magda opens the storeroom and switches on the light. It is dusty and there are spiders' webs all over the ceilings and between the bricks. The room smells stale and he is sure no one has been inside for years.

He is thankful he brought the newspapers as he can use them to create an area where their possessions can be placed. He busies himself laying them out, and Magda helps once she sees his plan. Soon they have laid out a square area roughly the same size as the back of the *bakkie*. The two of them carry the goods, line by line, in and place them inside the storeroom.

Once they have brought everything inside, they cover their belongings with the last remaining pieces of newspaper.

He takes a last look, breathes out deeply and, once he and Magda are outside, locks the door behind them.

"My child, your mother is supposed to come back with us. Please see if she has returned, give the key to Mrs. Visagie and thank her for me." He hands her the key.

"Okay, Pa. I will do that."

For the second time Magda disappears round the corner. He busies himself by dusting out the back of the *bakkie* before closing it.

Magda returns quickly, but her face is filled with confusion.

"What's wrong, my girl?" he asks.

"Pa, Mrs. Visagie was on the phone and said I must come back later."

"Well, my child, maybe Mr. Visagie is organising something at the bank. We can wait a bit. There is enough time."

He moves the *bakkie* onto the main street so that they can see the entrance of the 7-Eleven and know when Martha is back from wherever she has gone with Mr. Visagie. They sit in the *bakkie* and wait in silence.

The minutes move slowly and there is very little action. No customers go into the 7-Eleven and very few people walk past. He observes Magda who is deep in thought with her eyes glaring off into the distance. She has not uttered a word and her thoughts seem to consume her.

When they had so desperately wanted a child, they had prayed hard to the Lord and were eventually blessed with her. He had never thought he would ever be in the situation, he now found himself in.

All he could do was pray. But God had answered his prayers and Magda had come to save him, the coffee that she gave him was a sign from God above. But he prayed that in Cape Town they would find work quickly and start again.

The minutes move into an hour and then two. Hendrik looks at his watch and it is nearly four.

"Magda, please tell Mrs. Visagie that we will be back once we have given the keys to the agent."

Magda obliges and quietly opens the door. Unlike the inactivity of the last two hours she is back within a minute. She gets back into the *bakkie* without saying a word.

They drive towards the house and Hendrik feels he has to ask Magda to help him clean otherwise he will run out of time. He had already done most of the cleaning the day before, but there were still a few places that needed to be wiped down.

They park next to the house they have inhabited. The house that has sheltered them over the past months. The time in Wolseley will definitely not be the happiest that they have spent anywhere, but it is at least a place that they could call home.

Magda has opened the door and he goes round to the back of the house to fetch the broom and cleaning cloths. He thinks it is best to pack their belongings into the *bakkie* then sweep each room. He is on his way back with the broom when he hears Magda's desperate calling.

"Pa!" she shrieks, "Pa!"

He starts to run.

"Pa!" the voice is shriller, higher and more panicked.

He finds Magda in the bedroom he once shared with his wife. Magda is desperately looking around.

"Pa, Ma's bag is gone."

He looks beyond her face, searching for any clues. On the floor all that remains are some papers and an envelope. They must have been burgled.

"Magda, go and see if your bag is in your room. We must have been robbed."

She slowly walks out the room.

While she is out he glances at the papers on the floor. He hunches down to look at them.

The envelope is not rubbish as he originally thought. Inside are two letters, a letter addressed to Magda and one to him, enclosed in the envelope are a few R100 notes.

Hendrik

I wish it could have been different. I have gone to Welkom. For your brother's sake, please don't come. I gave Magda the choice, she chose you.

It is not signed, but it is her handwriting. It is a record of a thought. It is the record of a decision. The decision excludes him.

"Pa," Magda walks in with her bag in her right hand, "my bag is here."

She looks at his face and registers that something is seriously wrong. He cannot speak, he cannot move.

Stuck in his fingers is a letter addressed to her. She takes it. She reads the words.

She folds the letter and places it in her pocket.

"What are we going to do, Pa?" she asks him.

27.

"I'm on my way there now. No, as I promised you when you bought it, it is going to be vacant by tomorrow. Don't worry, all under control. Chat later, bye."

He narrowly avoids a bloody guinea fowl that has run into the road. He swerves at the last minute, causing the car next to him to swerve too. The man leans out the window and curses him. He puts up his hand to say sorry, but the man *pulls a zap* at him, and then roars off.

At the arterial road, he turns left and sees the signpost – Wolseley 1.

The visit one week ago had been promising. There had been some kind of garage sale at the time and the people from the informal settlement and a few locals were clearing out most things. He knew he wouldn't have to use force to get them out, they were going to go voluntarily. Just in case, he had called on Clive to meet him there. At six foot three he tended to scare people.

He parks outside the house on the road. Clive is parked there already, talking to his girlfriend on his phone. He waits for the call to end. "Clive, you check the place out and make sure everything is in order, while I get the keys."

They walk past the *bakkie* to the front door. The door is standing wide open.

He motions for Clive to go around the back of the house and he knocks on the open door. No one answers so he goes inside. The house is empty except for a bag on the floor in the lounge.

There does not seem to be any sign of life. Kitchen - empty, lounge - empty, bedroom one - empty, when he reaches the second bedroom he jumps back in fright. There on the floor are the daughter and the father just sitting – not saying a thing.

"Sorry, I did knock," he says.

They both stare at him blankly.

"Everything ready to go?" he doesn't want to lose momentum, or get into much of a conversation.

The father is the first to speak. "She is gone. Martha is gone."

"Sorry to hear that, is Martha your pet?"

"My wife," he spits back with venom in his voice.

"Sorry, *sjoe*, okay, sorry, didn't know her name."

Clive walks into the room and is also visibly shocked by the two people on the floor. "What's wrong?" he hears himself saying.

There is no reply to the question, only silence.

Kevin chips in, "Look, um...things are not looking up right now, but...I want to be clear...we need you to leave the house."

More silence.

Clive looks to Kevin and not getting any signal says, "Look. I don't want any trouble, okay." He thinks this is the most appropriate thing to say. "The owner needs the keys back."

The father stands up slowly and he takes his daughters hand and they walk like somnambulists out of the room. He watches the daughter pick up the bag from the lounge floor and drop the keys onto the front counter.

"Just watch what they do," Kevin says to Clive.

He thinks it is best to get the keys, lock up the place and come back early tomorrow. Then they will have gone, he can then see that everything is okay; he can't deal with this shit now.

He locks the back door from the inside. He then quickly walks through each room. There is nothing left. When he gets to the front door he meets Clive who has retrieved the keys from the counter.

"Did you ask if there were any others?"

"Yip, the lady had the other one, and well she's kind of gone."

"Let's lock up and get the hell out of here."

Kevin locks the door and he makes a quick exit for his car. Clive has already started his car and winds down the window. He turns the car around. He watches Kevin get into his car. He waves at the man and girl in the *bakkie*, but they do not wave back at him.

28.

He was really hoping not to have to make this trip again, but yesterday was a little too much for him and he couldn't properly check that all was okay. As he drives over the bridge and sees the three houses below he can't help noticing the *bakkie* still parked outside the house.

"For fuck's sake," he says aloud.

He parks next to the *bakkie* and rolls down the window.

The father is awake and sees him, but the daughter is sleeping. He hoots.

"Look here, you have to go. I don't want this to get ugly but unless you go now I am going to get the police."

The daughter is now awake, puffed face and eyes still full of sleep. The father sits and stares at him without saying a word and without any action.

He hears her say, "Come Pa, we must go, Pa."

The father looks at his daughter and she touches his arm.

"Please, Pa."

The engine of the *bakkie* starts. It drives along the road. Kevin watches it as it crosses the bridge into the main section of the town before disappearing from sight.

He lets out a big sigh. Wolseley.

Part 2- Bakkie

1.

Hendrik wakes up with a start and is disoriented. It takes more than a minute for him to realise where he is. His whole body aches and his muscles are throbbing from sleeping in cramped quarters. Sleeping in the back of the *bakkie* amongst the only goods they had left was their only option once they had driven to Cape Town. He had not even wanted to go but it was Magda who had said there was more chance for them there. 'Cape Town, a city?' he had thought, but he could not show defeat to his daughter who had remained calm through the whole episode.

Not once did she complain or even ask about her mother. No, she had been numb.

How did it get so bad, so quickly, he thought?

Hendrik feels a sense of panic as he suddenly notices that Magda is not in the back of the *bakkie*.

"Magda!" he yells. Frantically he opens the canopy and stumbles and half falls onto the ground. The front door of the *bakkie* opens and Magda emerges half-asleep, her eyes red and swollen and her hair in a mess.

"Pa," she says in a squeaky morning voice.

"Sorry, Magda, just woke up and did not see you and was worried," he finds himself moving towards her, taking her into his arms and cradling her like he used to when she was a child. She does not resist, she lets him rock her back and forth and take long deep breaths.

"I am so sorry, my child," he finds himself saying. "I am so very sorry."

"Pa, there is nothing to be sorry for." She gently touches the middle of his back with her hands as if appeasing a small child scared of the dark.

2.

Magda goes in first to the service station bathroom after her father insists. It smells bad, like people have urinated all over the floors and no one has cleaned it for a few days. She looks around the basin, which is speckled with pieces of hand soap and knows that at some point she needs to look up and at herself in the mirror.

When she does she is shocked, the person looking back at her is different and not the one she is used to.

She has tried not to think over the past day, the more she does the more she feels herself sinking.

She turns on the water with her right hand and squeezes the soap dispenser with her left, she lets the water run over her whole hand and lathers up a foam which she quickly administers up to her elbows. She then washes her face. She looks around expecting someone to come in at any point. She really wants to wash under her arms and genitals but knows it is not possible.

After brushing her teeth she looks at herself again. Who are you? She wonders.

3.

It is while Magda is washing herself that Hendrik starts to hit the steering wheel angrily. He had tried not to think about the situation they were in. He had prepared himself for the trip to Cape Town, living in the *bakkie* while they sorted themselves out, but the vision had always included Martha who would take care of the finer details.

She must have thought about it, after all she was the one that had suggested the option. She must have thought about how they were going to stay clean, how they were going to eat, the basics. And now she was not there.

The drive from Wolseley to Cape Town was the longest of his life. Magda did not say a word. She had looked straight-ahead for the entire journey. He tried to steal glances during the ride, looking for some solidarity in the drama that had unfolded. But there was simply the steely glance ahead, the teeth fused together so that the muscles in the mouth gave away what was happening beneath.

What did he need to do? Once they got to Cape Town, how were they going to live? This buzzed and buzzed around his head, shouting the obvious that they were in big *kak*.

And now here he was sitting in the parking area of a *petrol station*, the smell of chemicals in the air. The *boys*, filling up the cars and the rude lady inside the convenience store staring at him with hatred in her eyes. She had continued to stare so much that he had moved the car to another parking spot so that he did not have to look at her.

At least they could come to a *petrol station* if they needed to. They could use the bathroom and do some basic cleaning. He could not think of anywhere else that they could use to do the basics. But they would need to come late at night or early in the morning when no one else was around so that they could clean in peace.

This was all he could offer Magda, and so he had insisted that she go first so that he could watch the door to make sure no one else came in.

Damn that woman, damn her. The hatred bubbled away in him. Because of that fucking woman he was having to look at his child with shame. It was too late now for him to do anything, the shame burned in him like a toxic chemical all the way through his body, destroying all that came in its way.

4.

Magda looks at her father as he eats the sandwich he is sharing with her. There is no enjoyment in his face; he is simply eating it mechanically.

She was worried when she had returned to the *bakkie* to find him mumbling and hitting the steering wheel. He had continued even when she had got in. She had looked at him for ages, but it was as if she was not in the vehicle at all. Eventually she had shook his hand and he jumped in fright.

"Pa," she had said quietly, "it's your turn to go to the bathroom."

Instead of moving he had stayed in the *bakkie* not able to do anything. She closed her eyes and rested her head against the window.

Time went by, she didn't know how much had past, when he eventually opened the door and got out.

Her stomach grumbled in hunger, making gurgling noises, but she tried not to focus on what her body wanted.

Her father did not take long, and before leaving had bought a sandwich for them.

This was not without commotion as from the *bakkie* she could hear him screaming. He was shouting at the woman behind the counter and there was almost an altercation when the men who worked at the *petrol station* began to make their way to help her.

Magda had jumped out the *bakkie* and run into the shop.

"Pa," she yelled, "stop it."

Her father stopped yelling at the sight of her.

"Sorry, sorry, sorry…" she said to all the parties now present in the store.

One man, who worked there, took the sandwich which was lying on the counter and gently led her father and her out. It was when they were near the *bakkie* that he said, "It is time to go now."

She looked at his face, a face filled with concern, and the afterthought of sympathy. He handed the sandwich to her.

"Thank you," she had said, taking it slowly.

Her father had lost all the anger that was in him. He was standing, not attempting to get into the *bakkie*.

"Come, Pa," she had said as she opened his door and manoeuvred him in.

"*Sisi*, please go," the man said.

"We will, Mister," she said, no longer able to look him in the eye. "Thank you…"

She got into the *bakkie* and looking down at her hands simply said, "Drive Pa, drive."

5.

Hendrik was near the city centre at the beginning of the residential area within Cape Town. He had parked in the road in a parking spot.

"Magda," he heard himself saying, "we need to try and find work."

"Okay, Pa," she said looking at him.

"I don't know anyone in Cape Town," he mumbled, "so we will have to start here in town and see if we can find something."

She did not reply again.

6.

Magda was back at the *bakkie* still feeling wounded at the experience from inside the store.

She opened the door and slammed it shut behind her.

Hendrik got into the *bakkie* quietly and just sat staring ahead, this time the veins in his neck were bulging out because he had pressed his teeth so closely together.

"Pa," she said, "they were so rude."

Her father did not stir and she knew she had to wait until he was ready, which nowadays was taking longer and longer. She had waited sometimes for more than an hour for him to respond. During this time, she closed her eyes and played a movie in her mind. The movie was always the same - her family living in a beautiful house near the beach somewhere, the house was full of furniture like in the magazines and the refrigerator had so much food in it, they could feed an army. She had a white Maltese poodle, just what she had always wanted, her name was Fluffy and she loved Magda so much. In this particular daydream, Fluffy and her were walking on the beach together. There was no one else. Fluffy chased the seagulls and then came running back to her to remind her that she was loved...

"Magda…" her father began.

She looked at him and he had changed colour again, this time the pink had given way to grey.

"Pa," she interrupted without waiting for him to finish his own sentence, "what is a *CV*?"

He cleared his throat and said, "It's a document you record your work experience on."

"So why didn't you give him one?" she asked.

Hendrik did not immediately respond, but there was not the long wait like before.

"My child, who knows what one should bring with one in a situation like this. I never even thought about it." He sighed out a deep sound and then looked ahead and continued, "Who would have thought, who would have thought…"

Magda could not hold back the questions anymore and even though she knew her father was not okay, she had to.

"Pa, he kept talking about skills? What are those?"

"Enough, Magda," he said.

"Pa," she began gently, "I have to know if I am going to try and get work. I didn't understand what he wanted."

"It's what you can do, my child, it's what you can do."

He started the *bakkie* and Magda, about to carry on, was cut short as he quickly took a right into the oncoming traffic.

7.

Hendrik knew he had to target a white person. Maybe if he could just explain the situation to them, they would consider giving him a job.

He had found a small *kaffee* which was manned by a *coloured* lady but he had seen a white boss come in and bark orders at her. He sat in the *bakkie* outside the store until the man came out to leave.

"*Meneer*," Hendrik said not looking the man in the eye.

The man jumped back in fright.

"Sorry man," he said, "didn't want to frighten you."

The man had started to look at him strangely and Hendrik started rambling as fast as he could.

"Please, *Meneer*, I have just lost my job and I have a family to support and all I am asking for is a job, I will do anything you want, really, please...please... I am begging you."

"Sorry, nothing here," and the man quickly slipped himself into the car, started it and drove off, and before Hendrik even realised it - he was gone.

8.

"Pa, they don't have any jobs." For the first time she looked out the window and felt herself dipping. There was not much left in her.

"My child, you tried, that is all you can do."

"Well we have to do something, food does not grow on bloody trees!" she snapped back, not sure how it even came out, for she had no recollection of thinking it.

She only realised the damage she had caused once she looked at her father's face, it had gone white, all the colour had drained from it.

"Sorry, Pa." Her throat constricted as she said it and she wished she could take it back, but she couldn't.

It was too late. He had opened the door, closed it quietly behind him and walked off into the road.

The tear started its journey down the side of her face, a single tear travelling over the contours of her cheek. It divided and was soon joined by others, all intent on painting her grief visually for all to witness.

9.

Hendrik counts the money that he has left. They have not used much, but the money has to last and has to be saved so that they can eventually get a room, once they both have jobs. He carefully folds the notes and puts them back into the wallet that he keeps on himself at all times.

He has parked the *bakkie* one road up from where he parked it the first night. This is his strategy, he will move the car around so that no one will get suspicious and phone the police. For now this is their house and he has to do everything he can to make sure it remains safe.

Magda has been distant since their last discussion and only talks when she has to. She tells him she wants to go for a walk and he asks her not to. He is eventually begging her, but she opens the door and walks off. He wants to follow her but he has to let her be. He watches as she walks down the street, she does not turn left or right but carries on walking, in his view at all times. Secretly he knows she does not want to go far, just give them both space to think.

But the time when he is allowed to think is not a good one. It is filled with demons and darkness. He does not know what to do. How does he get a job, how does he get himself going again?

Something that seemed certain in Cape Town is not happening the way he thought it would.

In the far distance he can see Magda almost at the intersection where the restaurants and *kaffee* are, where he asked for the job, and then she disappears.

He starts to panic. He locks the passenger door, gets out the *bakkie* and then locks his door and hurries after her. He half walks, half runs in pursuit, all the time fretting between the *bakkie* and Magda, and the fear that something could happen to either.

What if he does not get to her in time? Or, what if while he is following her someone steals the *bakkie*? He looks to the point in the distance where Magda disappears and back to the *bakkie* like a wild man. He has become a wild man.

10.

The *bakkie*, their home, has become like a prison and Magda feels completely trapped in it. She cannot escape him, every minute needs to be a shared space, it is claustrophobic. She needs some space, some little space. Even her body is constantly reminded of the prison, aching and cramping in protest at the restrictions, having to contort her body to sleep, having to mould herself to hide from those looking in. It is more than a prison; it is a goldfish bowl too. Everyone can see in.

Magda is frantic, she needs to get away from her father so that she can make the phone call, but he wants to be with her at all times. She tells him she needs to go for a walk, but he starts going off at her. In the end she has no choice, and jumps out the *bakkie* under the pretence of needing time to think. She does not believe her ruse is going to work as he jumps out too, but then she yells to him that she needs time and he lets her walk. She knows there is a payphone at the *kaffee* and she heads in that direction, walking slowly.

What if her mother does not answer, what if she really is on her own?

She takes out the letter that her mother wrote and carefully dials the number. It does not ring for long and it is not her mother that answers, it is a man's voice.

"Hello...Hello...is there anyone there?"

She considers hanging up, but reason takes over. "Hello, Uncle, Magda here...is Ma there?"

He is as shocked to hear her voice, as she is disappointed to hear his.

"Hello, Magda," he sighs, "let me get her for you." There is a short silence followed by the bellowing voice of her uncle calling her mother, "Marttthhhaa, quickly the phone."

She hears the steps, from a far off distance, and they get louder and louder until the phone rattles as it is picked up.

"It's Magda," Magda can hear him saying to her.

"Magda, Magda, is that you?" the voice is filled with emotion.

"Hello, Ma," she says and before she can help it she is crying, then sobbing, then howling, the pain escaping her body in short, sharp bursts.

She cannot speak anymore and even though she hears her mother talking, she lets go of the phone. The dismembered receiver swings round and round.

She starts walking back to her father.

11.

Hendrik sees Magda re-appear up ahead of him, her face is red, there are tears running down her cheeks and there is mucous spilling off her face. Her extreme sadness etched in her appearance is a blow to his gut; he has never felt like this in his entire life. If he could die at this point, be taken away, he would take the option.

He stops and stands, waiting for her. Not sure if he must comfort her or let her be.

12.

"Just stay in the *bakkie*, Pa," there is no more anger in her voice, "I will go and ask."

She opens the *bakkie* door, her muscles in her legs cramping from sitting too long, and heads for the *block of flats*. She considers ringing the buzzers but then decides against it.

Two men emerge from the parking lot and start to make their way towards the front entrance.

"Sorry to bother you," she hears herself say, "but do you by any chance have any food to give me and my father? We are really hungry."

She looks the one man directly in the eye as she does this. He does not have pity in his eyes. He looks straight back at her.

Then just to reiterate, she says, "I am not asking for money, please just food."

The one man walks into the entrance, but the one who looks at her, stops turns to face her directly and says, "Sure, just wait here. I will bring you something, but I think all I have is bread and cheese?"

"Anything," she says.

"Okay, just wait here, I will be down in a second."

She had not expected this to go so well the first time. The man disappears into the elevator and is gone. She looks at *the flats*, the cars, the pavement, anything to pass the time.

He returns with a yellow plastic bag. It is full of food. He hands it to her.

"Thank you," she says, "thank you so much." She takes it and it is heavy.

He does not say anything in response. He returns to the elevator and disappears.

13.

He has noticed the other cars, the ones filled with security guards and other people intent on getting him out of the area.

They think he does not know that he knows, but he does.

The security vehicle has come down the road at least three times in the last hour. Each time, it slows down next to the *bakkie* and one of the security guards looks at him while they drive past.

Magda does not seem concerned, but he moves the *bakkie* after the third time.

Eyes, eyes, everywhere watching him, the eyes are after him, they see, they see him.

14.

She does not remember what day it is anymore. Her daily existence is made up of asking for food from others. She sleeps for long periods of time and does a lot of thinking, well not thinking: daydreaming rather.

She has considered calling her mother many times, but after the last time and the emotions that it caused, she does not think it is a good idea.

Her father has stopped talking that much; he simply stares and stares and stares.

The big part of the day is when he moves the *bakkie* from one road to another. He mutters and mumbles as if there is something scientific about the choice of road, or on which side of it to park the car, but if she thinks about it, it really makes no difference.

Her head gets heavier and heavier and she falls asleep against the glass of the window, the cold sensation rubbing against her cheek, reminding her of where she is.

15.

He thinks of the time he was in the military chasing the *darkies*, the *darkies* intent on killing innocent white families. He is running in a field, they are everywhere, he can sense them to his left and right; they do not make sounds and blend into the darkness.

He runs, he has to run, if he stops moving they will kill him.

The rest of the commando is lost; he is the last man running.

Running into the darkness.

A hand picks up a knife and slices his neck. He watches himself fall to the floor, he watches the gash in his neck seep blood onto his uniform, he watches himself slowly slip into death, falling further down the tunnel until there is nothing anymore.

He wakes up, his face squashed against the cold glass, saliva having slipped out of his mouth, forming patterns on the window where his head lay.

16.

Magda picks up the receiver, terrified to dial the numbers. She can't. She replaces it and steps away from the phone.

There is no one there to witness her actions and she waits a long time at the blue phone box, just staring at it.

She finds she is speaking aloud, she is telling herself to make the call, to just do it.

Before she realises it, she has the receiver in her hand and there is a ringing sound on the other side. She does not even remember taking out the number or dialing it. The voice that answers is that of her mother.

"Hello."

"Hi, Ma."

"My child, I am so glad to hear your voice," it is sincere and there is concern in the tone.

"Ma," she begins cautiously but then knows she will not react like she did last time, "we are in Cape Town."

"How are you, my child?"

"I am fine, Ma, Pa is fine too," she adds as an afterthought.

"I am glad to hear you are okay."

Magda waits, but her mother says no more.

"Ma, we have not found jobs and we still live in the *bakkie*..." Before she is able to finish her sentence her mother has begun crying.

In between the tears her mother blubbers, "Please come here, Magda, please just come here."

"What about Pa?" she asks already knowing the answer.

"He can look after himself," her mother interjects.

"Ma, you know he can't." She knows it is pointless to carry on the conversation and replaces the receiver without saying anymore.

17.

Hendrik has now moved to a different section of town, he feels too many people are watching. Magda still sleeps in the front of the *bakkie* and he sleeps at the back. Every night that they have been in Cape Town, someone comes to look into the window, to steal something. He makes sure to jump up and scare them away. As a result he does not sleep well.

The new part of town is filled with houses with high walls and barbed wire, but there are not as many security patrols here and he feels he can better disappear.

He guards the area at night, while Magda sleeps. He walks the streets ensuring that no one comes near. They had a big fight about it; she once woke up and saw him walking in the distance. She told him it was safer for him to be locked in the back of the *bakkie* than to be on the streets. She does not understand that this is a war and there were going to be no prisoners.

Tonight he notices nothing, the evening is dead quiet, there are no sounds from the houses, there are no cars and there are no other people on the streets.

He feels lonely tonight, he longs for the touch of a woman, a kiss, a caress, a hug. These ideas have to get out of his mind, and leave him, leave him now.

He walks back to the *bakkie*, quietly lets himself in so as not to wake up Magda and stares for hours at the roof of the canopy. The shape, the textures and the nothingness.

18.

Magda watches the man walk up the street, a bunch of wild flowers clutched in his hand. The man patiently goes from house to house, rings the bell and then waits, but no one opens the door or comes to the gate. He stands for a minute or more, and then moves on to the next house.

He is now at the *block of flats* where the buzzers for each flat are connected to one speakerphone. He pushes one buzzer after another. No one comes out; many must hang up because he then pushes again quickly.

He carries on. He looks at her and smiles, a big smile but filled with emptiness. He carries on walking.

She would like to speak to him but knows she shouldn't.

She watches him continue up the road until he disappears from sight.

19.

"Shoot man," he hears the voice say.

"Commandant, he must die," another says.

He has no more energy to run. His hands and feet are made of lead, he can no longer feel, not even his muscles respond.

He cannot even open his eyes, nor can he lift his head.

"Shoot me," he says, "just shoot."

The sound of gunfire echoes through the air.

He wakes up startled and disoriented. There is an explosion that sounds like gunfire again. He looks up and realises it is the *noonday gun* which has been fired. He is parked two streets from it and the sound is amplified here.

20.

The centre of town is quiet so it must be a Saturday or a Sunday. Magda and her father have parked in one of the main roads.

Magda has just been given R500 by a man, who could not make eye contact, after she had told her story to him. He had cleaned out his wallet and thrust the money into her hands before quickly hurrying off. She could not believe the amount of money and had counted the notes again and again. She dashed to the *bakkie* to show her father and he looked at the money in disbelief.

"What would you like to eat?" he asked her.

"KFC, Pa," she replied.

"Then let's go and get you some."

"Us, Pa, let's treat us," she replied cautiously.

The store is busy; there are people in queues waiting to be served. This is in direct contrast to the dead city outside, Magda thinks as she considers the food options. The last time she had KFC was in Welkom and the smells and sight of the chicken, lying piled up waiting to be packed, has caused her to salivate.

"Pa, what are you going to have?" she asks.

The effect of the KFC on him is not lost as he looks dreamily at the boards advertising the various combinations and specials.

"I...just don't know..." he stutters while not taking his eyes off the food in front of him.

They stand in line, obediently waiting their turn. The wait seems like a lifetime but eventually they are served and Magda cannot contain her excitement.

"Three pieces and *chips* and a coke, please Miss," she gushes at the cashier, "Pa, what are you having?"

"The same," he stammers, "the same, please."

The woman behind the counter rings up the items and barks, "Sixty rand and fourty cents!"

Magda is nervous and carefully unravels the R100 note that she had rolled into a small ball.

The woman grabs the note, pushes some buttons on the till and places the change in her hand so quickly, Magda is mesmerised.

She is about to ask a question, when the woman barks, "Next!"

Magda jumps back in fright into her father. She smiles and then giggles, "Pa, Pa, I am so looking forward to this."

"I can see that, my child," he says.

The server packs their trays and the pile of warm food is now directly in front of Magda. She slowly picks it up and carefully walks to an open table. Hendrik follows quietly behind, not sure what to do.

She hungrily attacks the food, not being able to fill her mouth fast enough with all the different flavours. Her father on the other hand eats slowly, processing each morsel with care. Magda has bulldozed through everything on her tray and her father has still not got to the *chips*. She eyes them hungrily.

"Have the *chips*, I can't eat them," he says to her.

"No, Pa. They are yours," she says, her voice betraying her true intention.

He picks up the packet of *chips* and places it on her tray. He does not say anything more, and she does not want to upset him.

"Thank you, Pa."

The initial voraciousness has disappeared and she eats the *chips*, one by one, in rhythm with her father's chewing motion.

There is nothing left on the trays but a pile of bones, stripped bare of meat and gristle.

Magda has licked her fingers clean and sucked on them multiple times, ensuring no trace of any foodstuffs or by-products.

They sit there in silence, content.

Magda feels exhausted after the experience and feels her head getting heavy with sleep. She is so happy though, so happy to have the food in her.

"Pa," she says, "we should go."

He says nothing and stands.

Magda looks down the street, confused. She thought he had parked the car on the same street that the KFC was on. Hendrik is also looking confused. "Pa," she asks, "where did you park the car?"

He points at the space where he thinks he did.

"We must have parked further down," she says looking confused.

"Did we?" her father asks.

"Must have, Pa."

"Hmm."

"Well the *bakkie* is not here," she points and looks to him.

"You are right, we must have parked it further up."

He does not move, nor does she. She cannot remember the exact spot where they had parked. She looks left and then right, and then at the spot her father is still pointing at.

"Okay, Pa. Stay here, I will quickly walk up the road to see."

He just stares at her.

Magda quickly moves up the block, but the *bakkie* is nowhere. The other side of the road has no cars on it, so it could not be there. She walks slowly back to her father. He has not moved and is still staring at the spot where he thinks he parked the *bakkie*.

"Pa, it's not up there," she motions to the spot where she has just walked to and back. It is then that the realisation sets in.

She feels like someone has punched her in the stomach.

21.

Hendrik is led by Magda through the streets. Sometimes she is unsure and then stops and asks someone passing by for directions.

"Sorry, Mister, but do you know where the police station is?" Hendrik does not engage, allowing her to navigate the way. He follows her, zigzagging through the open spaces, round buildings across roads and down alleyways.

They walk in one suggested direction then get conflicting information and head in another. Magda is getting more irritated and is rude to those she asks for help. Some just ignore her and carry on walking.

Hendrik sees the blue light above the building and points it out to Magda. "Police station, Magda."

Now that they are directly outside he does not immediately go in, instead he stands in silence looking at the door. Magda pushes him from behind into the building. He does not like police stations.

The police officer on duty is business-like when he hands them an affidavit to fill out. "Describe exactly what happened. Try to put down as many details as possible so that the insurance company can use the information to process your claim."

Hendrik looks at him as he briefs him, "The *bakkie* was not insured."

"Oh, I see," the officer replies. "Still fill in exactly what happened," he stands to leave, "I will be back in five minutes."

"Magda, please write," he asks her.

"Pa, I don't know what to say."

"Please, Magda, you are the writer."

Magda sits down and picks up the pen.

"Pa, you speak and I will write."

He sighs deeply; he cannot do this. "Please..."

He watches as she looks earnestly at the paper in front of her. Her head is locked into a frown and she then carefully starts to write.

He reads as she places pen to paper, forming each word carefully.

The bakkie was parked in the road outside the KFC. The bakkie is white, it has four tyres and a canopy. There was stuff inside the bakkie, two bags and some plastic bags. The bakkie is old and it has some rust on the back. We went to eat at KFC and when we came back the bakkie was gone. We looked everywhere for it. But the bakkie is definitely gone.

When she is finished she looks at him, "Pa, what else must I write?"

"Nothing, my child, nothing."

The police officer is nowhere to be seen. There is no one else in the police station and the silence is eerie. They wait not knowing what else to do. Hendrik cannot do much but stare, his mind has switched off and he plays music in his head to think about something else.

Magda sits quietly and says nothing. Her eye has started to twitch. He looks at her and is overwhelmed. He has so much anxiety and cannot even fathom what if the *bakkie* is no more.

The police officer returns and is startled to see them. "Sorry, was caught up in something."

Hendrik knew this meant he had forgotten them. He is about to say something when the officer takes the statement and begins to read it.

"A white *bakkie*," he reads aloud and then looks at Hendrik. "Was it parked in Adderley Street?"

Hendrik looks at him but says nothing.

He hears Magda softly say, "Don't know, Mister, the road where the KFC is."

"*Ja*, that's Adderley Street." He lets out a sigh and then says without any emotion, "The *bakkie* was not licensed and was abandoned. It was picked up and taken to the lot."

The rage takes over Hendrik, he feels his hands shaking violently and he points at the police officer, "That *bakkie* was not abandoned. It is mine. You have no right to take it...you need to give it back to us now."

The police officer has stepped back as Hendrik locks eyes with him.

"You can't just go and take whatever you want when you see it."

"Hey, Mister, calm down," the police officer says to him.

Magda hearing the tone of the man steps in and touches her father's back, "Pa, please." It has no effect.

"Don't *fokkin* tell me to calm down," he explodes. "Give me my *fokkin bakkie* back!"

The police officer slams the desk hard.

Magda jumps in fright and Hendrik is confused by the sound.

"If you don't calm down I am going to arrest you, do you hear me?" His finger is pointing at her father.

Hendrik is so angry he cannot speak, and each time he tries to open his mouth instead of words, phlegm, spit and noise erupts.

Magda looks at the police officer, "Mister, please we lost our house and we…um…we live in the *bakkie*, it's all we have."

The police officer looks at Magda, then at Hendrik, the words thawing his face.

"I should have shot your people when I had the chance!" Hendrik spits.

"Pa!" Magda reels back.

The police officer lifts his baton as if to strike Hendrik, but Magda is pulling him with all her strength out of the police station. He resists, he pulls too. But she gets the strength from somewhere and he finds himself dragged out on to the street.

He is standing once again outside, directly under the blue light.

"We should never have given this country back to you people!" he yells, "you take it all, you take it all from us!"

"Pa, please," she begs.

He will hear nothing of it and stands outside the station, defiant and yelling with all his might, "You thieves, you fucking thieves, take, take, take, take!"

Magda has covered her ears in an attempt to muffle the sound.

"FUCKING THIEVES!"

22.

Magda looks at the crumpled mass on the floor. Her father has collapsed onto the pavement and is jerking back and forth in sheer anger. The noise is disturbing her. She is torn about what to do.

"Pa, I am coming back," she says to him. "Please don't come inside."

She carefully opens the police station door and peers inside. The police officer is still there but he is agitated and speaking on his phone to someone else.

She walks up to the counter and waits for him to finish his call.

"Yes," he says, without looking at her.

"Mister, I am sorry about my father," she waits and her voice fumbles as she tries to carry on, "he has been through a lot."

There is no response or acknowledgement.

"Please, Mister, how do I...how does we...I mean how can we get the *bakkie*?"

The police officer stands up and kicks back the stool, "R850 fine to be paid at the city lot, identity book and driver's license." He walks into the office and is gone.

Magda is left alone in the police station. She looks around the walls, with the posters and the people and the plastic chairs and the tears come, they come to show her she is human.

Part 3-Unknown

1.

Magda sits close to her father. They are huddled together next to a flowerbed and protected from the street by a low wall.

Her mind is too busy considering problems, and there doesn't seem to be many solutions.

She cleans out her pockets, but not before ensuring there is no one around. She lays the contents directly in front of her. There is the pile of notes, the only money she has, and a folded up piece of paper, the one with her mother's number in Welkom.

She leans across to her father and feels into his pockets. Extracting money, the key for the *bakkie* and his wedding ring, which he cannot wear because it keeps falling off his now shrunken finger. She adds this to her pile.

Their entire existence laid out in front of them.

The key is a painful reminder of their current situation, the ring of the past and the small amount of money of their impending future.

"Pa," she says not looking at him, "I will keep everything in my jacket. My pockets can zip closed so nothing will fall out."

He does not respond. She was not expecting him to.

The sum of their lives now lies in her pocket.

2.

Magda sits on the bench and stares at her father. Since the outburst at the police station, he does not talk. He gurgles, he makes hideous faces but he does not talk. His body has become hunched and he cannot walk easily. She walks by his side to help him lean onto her for balance.

She begged him to speak, but he could not. He has had enough, she thinks. He does not want to talk anymore.

They sit on the bench. It is warm.

3.

Karel has recruited her to come to a place that offers food if you help out and attend a church service.

Magda is scared of Karel. He looks the most wild of all the men living on the street. His hair is all over the place. He does not speak nicely and spits a lot. Magda tried hard to ignore him, but then he had come one day and literally sat next to her, forcing her to engage with him, even have a conversation.

Karel spoke about a 'shelter' where you could sleep in a dormitory and not on the streets. But that would mean being separated from her father, so she had decided against it.

Instead she has agreed to go with her father to the centre. There she can work and get a plate of hot food.

The centre is chaotic with some white ladies in charge at the front and they tell the men to, "Go and stand there," or, "sit over here." There is one lady who is in control, everyone calls her Mrs. Malan and she is strict and scary. When she sees Magda and her father, she is taken aback and quiet. She looks Magda over carefully and then asks her, "How long have you been living..." she struggles to find the right words. Her eyes continue to look at her, "How old are you?"

"I am eighteen," she replies.

"I see," Mrs. Malan says, but she is not finished with the questions. "How long have you been living like this?"

"Like what, Mrs. Malan?" She is confused.

"No, nothing. Right then..." She occupies herself moving two chairs around and then goes to the other ladies.

They are busy setting up some coffee and tea. They talk quietly and every now and then, if Magda listens carefully, she can hear a word or two.

"Eighteen."

"No!"

"She is just a child."

"No, man!"

Magda does not know what to do, as this is the first time that she experiences this kind of gathering. Karel has not explained what to do in the 'in between' times, when there is no prayer, or food, or other things.

Mrs. Malan eventually notices her just standing with her father and walks over. She tells them the rules and then addresses her father only.

"Do you understand?" she exclaims.

Magda has to intercede, eventually, after Mrs. Malan looks flustered and expects responses.

"Mrs. Malan, my Pa does not like to talk anymore," she is expecting the lady to yell at her like she does at others, but instead she looks her in the eye and touches her on the side of her arm. She looks over her father and then nods without saying anything.

"All right just have a seat over there. Your father and you can stay and help out at the centre while the others go out to clean."

"I don't mind cleaning, Mrs. Malan, I want to help."

"That's okay, what is your name?"

"It's Magda," she says and then pointing at her father, "this is my Pa."

Mrs. Malan nods again and then motions to where they should go and sit.

She ushers her father to the seat and helps him into the chair.

The session starts exactly as Karel explained. The others, who have been there before, sign in and then attend the prayer service which includes a small sermon read by Mrs. Malan.

The ladies working there insist that Magda does not go out with the other men to clean, and are more specific about her father, who they say needs rest. The ladies huddle together to discuss them after Magda tries to persuade them otherwise, and she overhears one lady say, "It must be a stroke."

"She is so young."

"Definitely, damage to the brain."

Her father has not had a stroke, he is just sad she thinks. She is about to correct them but then thinks about not getting into trouble for eavesdropping. They really need this place and, as Karel says, it is easy work for food.

Karel comes and sits next to her. She wishes he would leave her alone, but then he was the one that had suggested they come here. He tells her that there are people following him, they try to find him but he is always one step ahead, he then says that he has lots of money but it's locked away for now.

Magda pretends to listen but also makes a point of looking around the centre so that she does not have to make conversation.

"Can't even sell the *Big Issue* – that market is controlled by the black people."

Magda is not sure how to respond to this statement.

"They rent a child, they wear their traditional outfits and bow and curtsy at the cars. People feel guilty so they buy."

Magda decides it is best to nod.

"Each corner is owned," he jeers, "try and sell a *Big Issue* on one of their corners, they come after you and will kill you if they have to."

Karel's eyes are wide and his pupils dilated. He reminds Magda of a zombie she once saw as a child on the TV. It had upset her so much that she needed to sleep with the lights on for weeks. Now the zombie sits just across from her.

Magda is unsure of what must be done. She wants to ask questions so that she can understand how the centre works, but she would prefer not to have to speak to Karel. She is worried that the more she speaks to him, the more he will want to be friends.

"Karel," she begins, "what do we do on a day when we are here?"

"Well for the men, we start by putting on our vests, we have to so the motorists can see us. Don't want any accidents. Then we clean the streets and pavements, make sure all of the litter is put in bins," then as an afterthought, "don't know what women do, though."

"Wouldn't I do the same as you?" she asks cautiously.

"You can't be carrying those heavy brushes and getting your pretty lady hands dirty," he half snorts, half laughs.

"Maybe I can carry something, a bag or some rubbish?"

"Maybe you can."

Karel is distracted as he greets a newcomer that is late this morning. She turns to her father who sits in the corner gently rocking himself back and forward.

"Pa," she says, "I am going to help today and when I get back, we can get some food, Pa. Pa, we are lucky, Pa. Mrs. Malan is very kind."

She leans over and takes his hand and squeezes. His hands are ice cold.

Mrs. Malan motions her to come over.

"I really need your help here today," the tone is different, kinder and softer.

"Sure, Mrs. Malan, anything I can do to help."

"We have too many vegetables to chop for the soup and need an extra pair of hands."

Magda feels needed.

While Mrs. Malan walks with her to the other women she says, "Please don't listen to everything Karel says. The *Big Issue* is for everyone and you might want to think about selling it. Okay?"

"Yes, *Mevrou*."

Magda is relieved to be in the company of women again. However, when she is there they are quiet and do not talk much to her. Not that they are mean or rude, just quiet. Mrs. Malan switches the radio on and they listen to songs and talk about the Cape.

At least she is able to watch her father. He sits in the chair at the back of the room. He is not as agitated here as he is when they are on the street.

She washes the vegetables and diligently chops them.

Mrs. Malan is watching the huge pots on the stove; the vegetables in them are boiling.

Magda collects the peels and leftover vegetables and places them in a plastic bag. She feels the eyes of the women on her back as she goes about cleaning up the kitchen.

"Can I make you ladies some tea or coffee?" she asks them.

"That's very nice of you," Mrs. Malan clucks, "but make some for your father first."

"I will."

4.

The days and nights are getting colder. Magda struggles to stay warm. Karel has shown her how to place a newspaper in the front of her clothes and behind them for this helps to keep out the cold, especially an icy wind.

Her father is the one who feels the cold the most and she is sure to wrap him up in the blanket she got from the centre.

He mumbles and moans but she wraps him up tight. Now that is it getting colder, she has taken Karel's advice and is sleeping in the back of a parking lot. Where there is this machine that works 24 hours a day, it helps to keep them warm if they lie underneath the pipes.

The sound of the machine is not pleasant and there is a constant droning noise, something that is not always possible to block out. She is getting better at sleeping. She can now sleep for three or four hours at a time. Tonight it is more difficult and she puts it down to the chill in the air.

She wakes up with a start; there are four of them, drunk and childish. They laugh and make a big noise. The one pretends to kick an imaginary soccer ball and the others roar with laughter.

"I am telling you, I kicked it straight into the goals!" he yells and does a fake run around like those soccer guys do on the television.

While he is running he sees her and stops.

"What do we have here?"

She looks away.

"Hey guys, come and see this."

The other three walk over and soon she is looking at four sets of eyes examining her with curiosity.

"Just leave me alone, okay," she says.

Her father has woken up and is looking around bewildered.

"Ooohhh, or what are you going to do?" More laughter. The one guy scratches himself down there.

Hendrik, completely agitated tries to stand up but falls back to the ground. He is neighing like a donkey.

They all laugh hysterically.

She does not say anything. But she creeps closer to the wall, closer to her father.

"Ha, I knew it, this is a cat, this is a pussy cat."

Hendrik is struggling to breathe. White liquid starts to escape from his lips as he convulses in spasms.

"Bwahahahhah."

"I am going to scream," she says.

"I might like that," he leers.

The security guard from the building across the road has walked over.

"Evening, gentlemen," he says, "it's time for you to go home."

"Fuck you."

"Mister, no need to be like this."

It is then that the security guard pushes the panic button and the alarm for the building goes off. It is enough to scare them, and the drunk four quickly disperse.

"Thank you, Sir," she says to the guard.

"These streets are not safe for you, *Sisi*."

"It's all we have," she says.

Her father is having a fit; he froths at the mouth and is rocking uncontrollably. She places his head into her lap so that he can have support. She rocks in rhythm with him.

The security guard sits next to them, quietly humming a traditional African song. He does not try to interfere.

At twenty-minute intervals, the alarm from the building across the road goes off, punctuating the air.

Lullabies and sirens.

5.

Magda has made a sign, Karel told her to. She writes:

Homeless, please help. Hungry and nowhere to live. God Bless.

She props it up next to her, but as they are not on the main road, there is not much action. She considers leaving her father here and then going to the *robot* and walking between the cars. Karel was right, there is a competition and she watches from afar as some, who try to steal a spot, are attacked.

She huddles closer to her Pa.

6.

Going to the centre twice a week is what Magda looks forward to. The ladies still don't talk to her much when she is there, but Mrs. Malan always asks her to chop the vegetables and she offers to make tea and coffee.

The ladies chat amongst themselves freely, share stories about family and friends, fashion trends, holidays. Towards her, however, they are guarded and do not ask about her stories, or about her family. They interact with her only about the tasks at hand or when thanking her for offering them tea or coffee.

She would like to talk to the ladies, but realises that they must find it awkward. She doesn't try too hard herself.

The reason she likes going to the centre is that her father is the most relaxed there. The four or five hours that he sits in the chair listening to the radio, is good for him.

Mrs. Malan called her aside on the second visit and said that while the others were out, Magda could use the basin in the toilet to wash herself and her father. Magda was embarrassed; she knew she was not as clean as she had been before... Maybe the ladies thought she smelt bad and had asked Mrs. Malan to speak to her. Since they did not have the *bakkie* it was difficult to use the public bathroom to wash. They had to look for one which was open and where they could sneak in. They did not have many clothes and now people treated them as homeless. They were stopped from going in before they even tried.

She was about to apologise, but Mrs. Malan touched her shoulder and said, "It's okay."

She had brought soap and shampoo for them to use and put it in the cupboard with the tea and coffee so that it was always available at the centre.

Then it is all over and they are walking back to the parking lot.

7.

The pain is intense. She feels a burning sensation in her arm and stomach. Then again. She comes out of sleep and right into the reality of a shoe being kicked into her stomach. She screams.

The pain is all over her body and throbs. She notices that she is bleeding above her eye, only because the blood has gone into it, blurring her vision.

The thud sound next to her is not good as she hears her father moan in pain.

Then there is silence.

"Pa, Pa, are you okay?" She cannot walk but only crawl to him. He is not bleeding on his face or any parts of the exposed body. He looks at her and starts baying. The noise is terrifying. He howls and spits and collapses as he tries to stand.

This time no one has come to help. There is silence on the street.

She cannot remember anything about the attacker: face, clothes or looks. All she can remember is the shoe. The big black boot that kicked her.

She needs to wash her face, but there is no water nearby.

"Pa, calm down."

Her father keeps trying to stand until she sits next to him and forces him down.

"Pa, you have to calm down."

He struggles some more but he does not have the energy to fight.

She takes a newspaper page and dabs her face with it. The blood has started to clot and dry. Above her eye is sore and her ribs ache every time she moves.

She lies down next to her father. He winces; he continues to wince throughout the remainder of the night. She cannot go back to sleep and nor can he.

8.

Magda cannot go to the centre today, even though she has not eaten and is hungry, her body is too sore to walk and she is feeling dizzy. She is waiting for Karel to come by so that she can tell him this.

Her father looks at his worst. He is a living corpse. He is gaunt, lifeless and his eyes are empty.

She sits upright, as this is the best position for her torso, although she is unable to stay awake and slumps against the wall.

She hears Karel before she sees him. He is talking to another man about the war, the war somewhere in a place called Rhodesia. When he turns the corner and sees her he goes quiet.

"What happened to you?" he asks in disbelief.

"Last night…some guy kicked us."

"*My Vader. Fok,* I am going to kill that fucker when I find him."

"Karel," she says, "I am not going to go today. I am too sore."

"I will try and get some food and bring it for you," he says the anger disguised. "I will ask Mrs. Malan for extra."

"Thanks, Karel," sharp pains shoot through her body and she closes her eyes and hugs the wall.

Maybe she is asleep, maybe she is awake. Maybe she is dead, maybe she is alive.

She drifts in and out of space.

Mrs. Malan is standing in front of her. She looks enraged. She screams and stamps her feet.

The cloth is cool, it wipes her face. It makes her feel good.

The soup is warm. It trickles down her throat and into her stomach.

Mrs. Malan is crying, her mascara is running down her face.

Run, run, and run. How the mascara runs.

Warm hands touch her face, gently circling her eyes and there is a smell, a nice smell.

Then she is flying, she is on the back of a *bakkie* and she is flying. She occasionally opens her eyes and the cool air stings her face.

But is her father on the magical *bakkie* ride? Is he a passenger too?

She does not know, she cannot see clearly.

And on they drive, the last image as they rise above the sea is a picture of the mountain, the big mountain in front of her, getting smaller and smaller.

9.

Mrs. Malan looks intently at her. She is not sure where she is.

"You are okay now," Mrs. Malan tells her.

"Where is Pa?" she asks unable to move her neck. There is a brace on it that prevents her from looking left or right.

"He is here, don't worry, he is here."

"Where are we?"

"You are at my house."

"Sorry, Mrs. Malan. I don't want to bother you."

"You are not. I have a *maid's* room which is not being used. You and your father can stay here. I will look after you."

"Really," she says in disbelief, it is too much and the tears come. She cries even though her body aches.

"You need to rest," she says and takes out two pills. She pours some water and makes Magda drink them. "Sleep now."

Magda falls asleep almost immediately.

10.

When Magda wakes up, she is warm and it is quiet. For just a moment she thinks she is in the house in Wolseley, but when she opens her eyes she remembers where she is.

Magda looks around the room and at the form of her sleeping father. He is breathing heavily and must be in a deep sleep. She quietly opens the door and slips out.

She is careful to open the outside gate so that is makes no noise and does not bother anyone.

The streets in the early morning are completely abandoned and she walks briskly enjoying the cold air on her face. It has rained for two weeks, solid grey rain, but today it has stopped.

The puddles of water lie all over the pavement and as she walks she skips to avoid them.

The phone booth is located in a park. This booth is clean and the phone looks newer and like it has never been used. She reaches into her pocket and extracts the folded slip of paper. She picks up the receiver and inserts two coins into the telephone and carefully dials the number.

There is no ringing sound. Instead she hears:

"The number you have dialed does not exist, dial again carefully or refer to directory enquiries."

Her clumsy fingers, she thinks. This time, with extra care, she dials ensuring to evenly hit the number with one finger at a time.

Again there is no ringing sound, "The number you have dialed does not exist, dial again carefully or refer to directory enquiries."

After a third attempt, she replaces the receiver and hears the coins being returned.

South Africanisms

Bakkie - pickup truck (Afrikaans)

BEE - black economic empowerment

Beeld - Afrikaans newspaper

Big Issue - magazine sold by homeless people

Blerrie - 'Bloody' (Afrikaans)

Block of flats - apartment block

Bond - a mortgage

Braai - 'barbecue' (Afrikaans)

Chips - french fries

Coloured - a mixed race classification, differentiating between black African and a mixture with some other race, normally white.

CV - curriculum vitae or resume

Darkies - derogatory term for black people

Fok - 'fuck' (Afrikaans)

Fokkin - 'fucking' (Afrikaans)

Ja – 'yes' (Afrikaans)

Kaffee - 'small convenience store' (Afrikaans)

Kak - 'shit' (Afrikaans)

Maid - a term used for a black or coloured female servant

Meneer - 'Mister' (Afrikaans)

Mevrou - 'Mrs.' (Afrikaans)

My Vader - 'My Father,' could also refer to 'God' (Afrikaans)

Noonday gun - cannon fired in Cape Town at 12pm

Petrol station - gas station

Please call me - a free text message to get the recipient to call you back

Pulls a zap – to show the middle finger

Robot - traffic light

Sisi - 'Sister' (Xhosa)

*Sjo*e - 'oh' (Afrikaans)

Skinner - 'talk behind ones back' (Afrikaans)

*Snackwich machi*ne - sandwich toaster

Tannie - 'Aunty' (Afrikaans)

The *boys* - derogatory term referring to menial workers normally of colour

Township/location - informal settlements where people of colour in South Africa were sent to stay during the apartheid period (still exist today)

Veld - 'savannah' (Afrikaans)

Waterblommetjiebredie - is a stew and literally means 'small water flower stew' (Afrikaans)

Gratitude

A storyteller is not a singular person; a storyteller is a combination, a moulding together of fine human beings who are willing to teach, inspire or simply foster that creativity. The following is a list of some of those:

Beryl Lavender

Audrey Stockdale

James Downham

Steve Elkington

Ilona Louw

Enrico Gerber

Ken Shuter

Andrew Daniels

Sue Tarr

Yvonne Banning

Joan Hambidge

And to those whose names I cannot remember, but are as much a part of this journey, this work is yours too.

164

This book is also dedicated to the two wonderful women who shaped my life, for whom I am truly thankful and for whom I miss terribly - Margaret and Nina.

And for the two wonderful men who continue to inspire me: Hoon and Wessel.

Thank you to Jean Spencer-Young, Glynnis Newdigate, Sam Newdigate and Tanya Barben for the initial work on the manuscript.

To the team at *South Africa Writing*, thank you for this opportunity.

About the Author

J. John le Grange studied creative writing at the University of Cape Town under novelist Joan Hambidge. He was a place winner in the 2000 Seoul Creative Writing competition and briefly edited *South Africa Writing*, a magazine for creative writers. He lives in Cape Town.

CPSIA information can be obtained at www.ICGtesting.com
Printed in the USA
LVOW10s2343260116

472427LV00015B/209/P